CONCEALMENT

A BROOKE HILL NOVEL

A.E. LEE

Cover & interior design by Typewriter Creative Co.
Cover photos from Dreamdes / Adobe Stock

ISBN 979-8-9923693-5-9 (Paperback)
ISBN 979-8-9923693-6-6 (eBook)

To my beautiful big sis, our very own Aunt T

CHAPTER 1

The small room in the Fairfax County Government Center was packed, the hot stale air made it hard to breath. Brooke's small division of the Fairfax County Police force was about to get their newest detective, and she was about to get her first partner in the domestic violence unit.

Brooke took her seat on the blue metal folding chair next to her boyfriend and fellow Officer, Nick Simons. She gave a quick wink to her new partner, Dan Beal who was standing next to his very pregnant wife Kat and their three towheaded little girls. *There was truly not a more beautiful pregnant woman than Kat,* Brooke thought to herself. Long blonde wavy hair and a beautiful glow to her skin, which was always there, pregnant or not. Brooke noticed Kat looking lovingly at her husband as he raised his right hand. *I hope that is the way others see us;* Brooke squeezed Nick's hand.

Sergeant Jeff Willows who'd sworn Brooke in four years ago was now about to swear her partner in. Dan was one of the nicest people Brooke has ever met, man-bun and tattoos and all. Beal looked and sounded nervous as he repeated the words Brooke herself had recited.

"Repeat after me: 'I, Daniel Barry Beal'..." Willows' deep voice reverberated through the small space.

"I, Daniel Barry Beal . . ." Dan's voice wasn't the only one to repeat the phrase, Dan's young daughter Ellie whispered it as well, although not quietly enough. Laughter filled the room as everyone heard her sweet little voice. With a quick word from Kat, Ellie sealed her lips and smiled at her dad.

"Do solemnly swear to continue upholding the laws of the land, to protect and defend, and to serve . . ."

Tears formed in Brooke's sapphire blue eyes. Nick, having noticed, handed her a tissue. "Are you okay?" he whispered in her ear.

Without hesitation Brooke looked into Nick's deep brown eyes and said, "I want what they have." It was Nick's turn to squeeze Brooke's hand. Then he whispered, "Me too, Hill."

Applause erupted and broke Brooke and Nick out of their trance. "Yay Daddy!" All of Dan and Kat's girls yelled.

Brooke and Nick made their way to the front to congratulate the new detective.

"I'm so happy to be sharing my shoebox office with you, partner." Brooke hugged Dan.

When they separated, Dan replied, "In all seriousness Brooke, thank you. If it wasn't for your push this wouldn't have happened." Dan stepped back and she could see his sincerity.

As Brooke turned to make way for other well-wishers she spotted her boss, Lieutenant Sheila Adams, a tall and lanky black woman with a contagious smile. She nodded to Brooke, a sign to go over.

"Well done Detective Hill. Detective Beal is going to make an excellent partner for you. Our community is lucky to have you both fighting for what is good and right."

Brooke smiled as she looked on at her new partner. Lieutenant Adams continued. "I've just gotten word that we have two officers requesting the domestic violence detective," she paused and smiled. "Excuse me, detectives."

"I'll head out now." Brooke turned to find Nick in the crowd and let him know she would meet him back at her place.

"Detective Hill, let's let your partner have his moment. I think you can handle one last call by yourself," Lieutenant Adams turned to greet another guest.

Brooke found Nick standing against the wall, his head was down, concentrating on his phone.

"Are you looking at memes again?" Brooke teased as she put her arm through his. Nick looked startled at first. He gave a half smile and put his phone away quickly.

"Ready to go beautiful?" He kissed her cheek gently. His touch gave Brooke butterflies, a feeling she hoped would last forever.

"I was just talking to Adams, there was a DV call just now, and they are requesting that I go." While Brooke loved her job, she was disappointed to not fully take advantage of her day off.

"Not taking your new partner?" Nick asked gesturing with his head to Dan who was still taking pictures with his family.

"I think he deserves to have this moment; one last call won't kill me."

Nick nodded his head. "Good thing we met here then. See you back at your place later?"

Brooke hugged him. There were few words to describe how it felt to be in his arms, engulfed in a hug, safe was the only one that came to mind. She kissed him and pulled back to look into his eyes. "See you soon Simons."

"Be careful Hill."

CHAPTER 2

Brooke pulled up to the small yellow rancher just as dusk was touching the sky. The brilliant shades of pink, blue, and purple danced around in the heavens. Brooke looked up and took a moment to take it in before proceeding up the walkway. She pushed the dilapidated iron fence gate opened and proceeded to the white front door. Brooke noticed right away the camera that was pointed at the front door. She looked towards the garage and noticed another camera. As she raised her hand to knock, the door was opened by one of the two responding officers.

Officer Pitt was tall with a buzz cut; he extended his hand to shake Brooke's as he greeted her. "Detective Hill, thank you for coming," he looked behind her as he took his hand back. "Beal not with you?"

"No, I came straight from the ceremony, he was still held up there. I'll brief him after." A loud bang followed by a mix of Spanish and English made Brooke peer into the slightly opened front door. She could only see the other officer's back.

Officer Pitt closed his eyes before beginning to speak.

"This has been going on for about an hour and half now. They demanded to speak to someone in charge." Officer Pitt made air quotes with his hands as he said in charge.

Brooke gave a puzzled look as he continued. "Victim is Catalina Dorado Hall, inside with her Aunt Maria Alvarez. Catalina is saying that her husband Matt Hall has a history of abuse. Catalina was just taken by ICE agents and held in Farmville for twenty-four hours. The call came in because Catalina believes Matt is now stalking her." Officer Pitt paused for Brooke's reaction; he wore a look of utter exasperation on his face.

"Right. Guessing that she has no actual evidence as to what is happening and that is why there are raised emotions in there." Brooke gestured towards the inside of the house.

"Yep. Officer Gonzaga threatened to arrest the aunt if she did not calm down. I think they thought they could just call us out and that would be that." Officer Pitt crossed his arms and turned his attention once more to inside the house where voices were raised again.

"No sign of physical abuse or anything amiss on the property?" Brooke was looking around at the front of the house.

"Nothing. There does seem to be real fear from Catalina, but we have nothing concrete to go on." Brooke started to step in front of Pitt and grabbed the front doorknob.

"I'll take it from here. If you and Gonzaga can wait out front, I'll talk to Catalina and her aunt alone inside."

Brooke took a step inside the house as she heard Pitt say roger then the crunch of gravel under his foot.

"Officer Gonzaga," the officer turned his attention towards Brooke. He was the opposite of his partner, short, longer dark hair. The feeling of frustration from him was palpable as he approached Brooke. "I just spoke to Officer Pitt, if you wouldn't mind waiting out front. I will talk to Mrs. Hall and Ms. Alvaraez." He whispered thank you and quickly passed by Brooke on his way outside.

Breathtaking. That was the only word to describe Catalina Dorado Hall. Brooke was pretty sure she had never seen a more strikingly beautiful woman. She wore her long, beautiful, light brown hair in a low ponytail that cascaded down her back. Catalina was standing next to her aunt who bore a striking resemblance to her, just an older version.

"No one believes her!" Maria pointed her finger towards Brooke's face. Catalina put her hand on her aunt's forearm.

"I'm sorry..." Catalina trailed off not knowing what to call Brooke.

"Detective Hill, I am one of the domestic violence detectives." Brooke extended her hand to shake Catalina's.

"Thank you for coming. I apologize for the raised voices; we are just very frustrated by this whole thing. We thought calling the police was the right thing to do, one of my uncles is a police officer in Maryland." Catalina was cut off by her aunt yelling in Spanish.

"I understand!" Brooke yelled over Maria hoping to

11

be heard. This made both women stop and look at her. "I understand," she said more quietly now. "This can be very frustrating, and I know you are scared. What Officer Pitt and Gonzaga were trying to explain was that we can't do anything really without proof. Something tangible. A photo of previous abuse or stalking? Video footage from the security cameras outside? Anything we can see that prompted you to call today? Does that make sense?"

Both women began speaking in Spanish again to each other. Catalina stopped to address Brooke. "The camera does not take video, but my cousin Carlos has some photos of my husband as he has been spying on me. I can get them to you tomorrow."

That struck Brooke as odd. *Why not right now?* "Ok, can you come by the station tomorrow? I can look at the photos and take an official statement."

"Yes, but what about her son." Maria was calmer now but still openly hostile to Brooke.

"I'm sorry I didn't know there was a child involved. Is he here?" Brooke looked around and saw no evidence that a child lived here.

"No, my husband is keeping my Mateo from me. He told me when he picked me up from ICE that I could no longer live in my apartment or see my child." Catalina began to weep at the mention of her son, Maria put a consoling arm around her and glared at Brooke.

"I think our best course of action is for you to come to the station tomorrow, I'll be in after eight. We can put you in touch with some resources that can help with getting your son back. I'm sorry, I know this is difficult, but nothing is going to happen tonight unless you can prove that you or your son is in immediate danger. Do you believe your son is in immediate danger?" Brooke leaned forward towards both Catalina and Maria.

Maria opened her mouth, but Catalina spoke first. "No. He's not. We will come by tomorrow morning. Thank you, Detective." Catalina turned to Maria who scowled at her.

Brooke gave both women her card and turned to walk out. She was greeted by both Officer Pitt and Gonzaga. "You and Maria besties just like we are now?" Gonzaga asked.

"I would never want to steal a friend from you Gonzaga," Brooke playfully hit his arm. "They are coming by the station tomorrow morning with more evidence. Thank you both for calling me." Brooke walked to her car and waved her hand behind her head to say goodbye to the two officers. She pulled out her phone. There was a photo of Nick, shirtless in her bed.

Hurry home Hill.

CHAPTER 3

"**U**gh," Brooke groaned as her favorite song "Africa" by Toto blasted through her alarm at 5 a.m.

"You've got to change your alarm," Nick grumbled into the pillow next to her. He shifted onto his elbows and kissed her. Even at this ungodly hour he was beautiful. The Ohio native could have passed for a cool California surfer with his mop of blond hair. "Or I have got to stop staying over on my days off when you have to work."

"Well, that is not an option," Brooke said before she kissed him back. "And how dare you diss one of the greatest songs by one of the greatest bands ever." Brooke playfully shoved him off his elbows.

"Greatest bands ever? Name another song by them." Nick said with a smirk.

Brooke loved the challenge, and the flirtatious banter. "Hold on, let me just check my ph.."

"Nice try Hill, but no googling." Nick snatched her phone out of her hands. "That's cheating."

"Hey!" She grabbed his wrist as they engaged in a playful tug-of-war. "Okay, fine. You win, but that is my song and my favorite way to wake up."

"Favorite way?" Nick said, with another one of his trademark smirks.

"Well, one of..." Brooke wrapped her arms around his neck and kissed him.

"How about I give you another, much more fun way to wake up?" And with that Nick tangled Brooke up in his arms and legs under the covers.

* * *

After Nick made good on his promise to wake her up better than her alarm, Brooke stared breathless at the mini chandelier above her bed.

"That was.." She gazed at Nick.

"Yeah.. it was." He turned smiling at her. "How about you take the day off? We can hang out all day just the two of us. Turn our phones off and just spend the day together."

"Hmm... sounds like you are trying to escape something there Simons." Brooke propped herself on her elbows, her long brown hair cascaded over her face and shoulders. Nick pushed a few strands out of her eyes.

"Who isn't?" Nick kissed her. "Plus playing hooky all day with me... come on Brookie doesn't that sound fun?"

"It does, but I can't." Brooke yawned and rubbed her eyes. "Beal and I are just wrapping up the Blueberry Hill case. We have to finish the paperwork and go over the details this morning and I also still have to brief him on the call from yesterday before they come in."

"Suit yourself Hill. Your loss." Nick tossed his pillow at her.

"I would if I could. I really would you know that." Brooke kissed Nick one more time before climbing out of bed.

Nick's phone began to ring as her feet hit the floor. He grabbed it and looked confused. Brooke couldn't help it and tried to sneak a peak at who was calling him.

"Everything okay?" She fumbled for her glasses and then her bra.

"Yea, just not something I want to deal with." He ran his fingers through his hair. That was his tell for when he was stressed or worried about something.

"Are you sure you're alright?" Brooke could see the look of concern on Nick's face.

"Yea, it's just..." They got interrupted by his phone buzzing again. "I should take this. I'll be in the kitchen." Nick jumped out of bed, ran to the bathroom, and pulled a towel around himself. He took a deep breath and opened the bedroom door. "Hello?" Then he disappeared.

Brooke was left standing in her underwear alone. She knew something was up. She tried to push the questions out of her mind as she got dressed. It was no use; the overthinking had begun. Was it work? Family? Ex-flame? She couldn't help the nagging feeling that it was a female on the other end of the phone with him. Given Nick's rotation of women before they had decided to be more than friends, she felt it was understandable to harbor these thoughts.

Once fully dressed with her contacts in Brooke walked out into her sunlit bright white kitchen. Nick was nowhere to be found. She padded across her engineered hardwood floors in her bare feet then checked her mudroom that leads into the carport. She heard the faint muffled sound of Nick's voice. Brooke put her ear up to the door.

"What do you want me to do?" Brooke could hear Nick saying.

"Okay. Yeah. Let me know." Brooke knew that was her cue that the conversation was over. She sprinted into the kitchen and started fumbling with the ancient coffee pot she had inherited from her Aunt Talia, Aunt T, as she was affectionately known as to Brooke and her younger sister Cassie. She could always afford to get a newer one, a fancier one, but this antique fire engine red coffee pot held sentimental value. Even if it was an eyesore.

Brooke was banging on it to get it to start working when Nick walked into the kitchen. "At some point it might be time for a new one of those," he said as he pointed at the coffee pot.

"First my favorite song, and now my coffee maker? So hurtful Simmons." Brooke spun around as she said this. She was about to embrace him in a hug to play off her eavesdropping but stopped dead in her tracks. Nick looked like he had just seen a ghost. His normal sun kissed skin had gone skeleton white.

"Are you okay?" Brooke put her hands on his forearms.

"Yeah, I'm fine." Nick was trying to play it off like nothing was wrong. Brooke knew better and gave him a knowing look. Still, he continued to divert. "I just needed some fresh air. I don't think what we ate last night sat well with me." Nick rubbed his stomach.

"Oh, yeah I've felt off too this morning." Brooke played along. She knew something was up and whatever it was, she assumed it must be serious... especially with him getting a call before 6 a.m. But what would he keep from her? What could be going on that he didn't feel comfortable saying it outright?

"I'm going to jump in the shower and then just head home. Try and sleep whatever this is off." Nick turned towards the bedroom, still wrapped in her pink fluffy towel.

"Okay, sure. You sure everything is okay? Who was on the phone?" Maybe prying would get him to talk to her.

Nick turned back to look at her. "It was just my dad; you know how stressed out he can make me. Nothing earth shattering just bugging me to visit. Love you Hill." He turned back around and disappeared down the hall.

"Love you too."

CHAPTER 4

Brooke pulled out of her carport in her white Camry. She looked back in her rearview mirror at her ranch style house. She loved this house. The gray brick house with black shutters was perfect for her. The only thing she had done after she moved in was paint her front door red. Her sister Cassie had read somewhere that having a red door brought you luck. After staring at paint colors for hours, Brooke conceded and has always been happy she did. She also loved seeing the blue pickup truck parked in the driveway as she drove away, a reminder that Nick and she were officially together. Seeing it there still made her heart skip. They had been together for six months now, without so much as fight, but Brooke couldn't shake the feeling that was about to change with Nick clearly keeping something from her.

What could be going on in his life right now that would make him lie to her? The overthinking was hitting its peak as she drove down Fairfax County Parkway. She was only a few minutes away from the station, but Brooke knew she couldn't start her workday like this. It would be all consuming all day, and she would be useless to those who needed her – her partner, the public, everyone. She was distracted. She needed Cassie.

Cassie Hill had always had a larger-than-life personality. It was no surprise to anyone when the minute she could, she packed up everything she owned and headed to the Big Apple. After struggling to make it as a Broadway star for five years, Cassie had just landed her first big role as William Shakespeare's wife Anne in *& Juliet.* Nick and Brooke had gone up on her opening night last month, Brooke could not put into words the pride she felt for her baby sister. The public thought so to, Cassie's portrayal of Anne was met with rave reviews.

Brooke glanced at the clock. It was just after 7 a.m., still a little early to call a night owl, but she was sure Cassie would consider this a sister emergency.

With just one ring Cassie appeared on the FaceTime call. "What's wrong?" Cassie asked without even a hello. Her bedroom was engulfed with light, her brown curls looked unruly on top of her head. Cassie's eyes were just as blue as Brooke's, but the red around them gave away that she had been crying.

"I think I should ask you the same thing. Are you okay?" Brooke said. She had just pulled into her parking spot at the station.

"I'm fine," Cassie could barely get out before tears came down.

Brooke stared sympathetically into the phone.

"I had one of those dreams." *One of those dreams.* Cassie

and Brooke had been having those dreams since they were little girls, when little world came crashing down.

It always amazed Brooke how if she closed her eyes she could recall the details of that night. The sound of her parents screaming at each other, the smell of the gasoline, the heat of the fire that ended up claiming both their parent's lives. The visions, the dreams, came back to Brooke too, more often than she would like. She always supposed that it was because of her line of work, working on cases that so closely mirrored her own experience with domestic violence. It was her reason for becoming a police officer. Until now, she hadn't known Cassie still experienced them too.

"Oh Cass, I am so sorry. I didn't know you still had those dreams." Brooke couldn't remember the last time she heard of Cassie having one.

Cassie blew her nose. "Every once in a while. Normally when something reminds me of Mom and Dad."

"What do you think brought this one on?" Brooke took her phone out of her car phone holder so she could see Cassie better.

"Last night walking home from the show, there was this couple that was arguing. The man grabbed the woman's arm. Just the way he did it, it reminded me of something I saw Dad do once." With that Cassie began to cry again.

Brooke knew the move. Her father used to grab the upper part of their mother's arm to turn her to face him, so he could spit more venom at her. Brooke closed her eyes for a brief moment visualizing the scene from her childhood.

"Why didn't you call me? You know you can call me anytime, it's not like I don't understand. I still have the dreams too." Brooke looked sympathetically into the FaceTime, willing her sister to look into her eyes, to understand how much she meant what she said.

"I know. Please don't be offended but I called Aunt T."

Aunt T was the closest thing to a mother they had. Being her mother's only sister, she willingly gave up her glamorous life in California and returned to Springfield, Virginia to raise her young nieces. Brooke pictured her Aunt T now with her toffee-colored hair swept up in a high bun and her red glasses practically falling off her nose. She understood why Cassie would contact her, even if it did sting a little to not be the first phone call.

"Don't worry about offending me. What can I do? I hate seeing you like this Cass." Brooke hoped she sounded sincere for sisterhood's sake.

"I'm fine. Honestly. Really, I am. I'll make some tea and put a face mask on then take a nap before I have to head back to the theater." Cassie shook her body and rubbed her eyes. "Ugh. Okay, let's talk about you. What's going on? Why did you call me this early?"

Cassie was getting up and started walking around her sunlight studio apartment. With her new big role, it afforded her to have a place of her own, instead of her Brooklyn third floor walkup with three other roommates. She had decorated it with an eclectic mix of antiques and Pottery Barn. All of a sudden Brooke was staring at a brick wall.

"Um, Cass I can only see your wall." Brooke made a face as she looked at the time. She had pulled into her normal parking spot five minutes ago and really needed to get into the station.

"Sorry, one sec. Just putting the tea pot on to make some tea." Cassie yelled from what seemed like across the room. Then her face was in the screen again. "Okay, all yours. Start talking."

"This feels stupid and childless to talk about now. It's Nick. He is acting weird. He took a phone call this morning early, like before six, and left the house completely to take it. When he was back, he was not himself."

"How not himself?" Cassie reached for a teacup.

"Stressed. He was clearly stressed. And when I asked him what was going on he lied to me. Told me some story that it was his dad and then left to take a shower. It was just.." Brooke couldn't find the words for it, but she didn't have to. Cassie did.

"Weird." Cassie looked down as she placed her teabag in her cup.

"Yeah, and my mind began to just spin, and the over-thinking was too much. I know he is lying to me. And I don't get why he thinks I would buy anything he was sayingggg....ah!" Brooke jumped at the tap on her window.

"Oh my God what's wrong?" Cassie said in alarm.

Brooke rolled down her window and her new partner

Dan Beal peaked his head through. "Hey Cass, sorry for scaring you both," he said with a laugh.

"Glad to see the man-bun is still in tack." Cassie thrust her teacup toward the phone as a way to say, cheers!

"You about ready to go in and debrief about the Blueberry Lane case?" Dan was still laughing at the two of them, even as he nudged Brooke to work.

"Be right there. Let me just finish with this one." Brooke nodded her head towards the phone.

"Right, see you in there." Beal turned to leave.

"Tell Kat I said hi!" Cassie yelled as Brooke rolled the window up. "Okay look, I know you don't have a lot of time so let me say this to hopefully ease your mind. There is no way Nick is going to mess this up. He waited too long for this," Cassie put her cup down to motion with her hands. "To be a *thing*. If he lied there is a reason. Give him the benefit of the doubt. Trust him Brooke. He's one of the good ones."

"I know." Brooke did know this. It was just, something didn't seem right. Her gut was telling her something different than the logical part of her brain. Brooke was lost in her thoughts when Cassie got her attention.

"Um, hello?" Brooke jumped startled again. Cassie started blankly staring at her through the phone.

"Sorry. You are right. Thanks Cassie. I just..."

"Needed to hear it. I get it. You better get in there. Don't keep your new partner waiting." Cassie's smile widened through the phone.

"Thanks Cass. Love you."

"Right back at ya." The FaceTime call ended. Brooke shut the door to her Camry and walked into the station, desperately hoping she would be able to silence the doubts invading her head.

CHAPTER 5

Brooke pulled open the double doors to the station and was greeted by June, the station dispatcher. The first thing people noticed about June was her warmth. She had the uncanny ability to make you feel right at ease as soon as she smiled at you. The second was her Mary Poppins English accent. June looked up from her desk and pushed a silver hair strand from her face. "Detective Hill, good morning! I don't suppose I could ask a favor of you?"

"Of course, June, anything." Brooke leaned on the top of the desk. She was trying to sniff the air for the aroma of coffee, having never actually accomplished getting a cup herself this morning.

"We have received two phone calls for Officer Simons this morning. The person doesn't leave a name or number but sounds quite panicky. I said he was not scheduled today on both occasions, and they quickly said they would try his cell and hang up. It sounds urgent, and I just want him to be aware. I was about to call him myself when you walked in." June pushed the same rogue silver strand of hair behind her ear.

"That's odd." Brooke was trying not to overthink the coincidence of these phone calls, and the one Nick received early this morning.

"I didn't mean to worry you dear." June placed her hand over Brooke's on the desk and squeezed to emphasize her words.

"No, it's fine, I am sure everything is fine. I'll let Nick know. Thanks June." Brooke turned and hurried past her not wanting to continue the conversation for fear of how she might react. *Remember, he is one of the good ones.* Cassie's words rang in her head.

As she rounded the corner and walked into her office, she couldn't help but laugh. The office was tiny to begin with and even smaller now that it had two occupants. The facilities manager had removed the extra chairs and squeezed another desk in for Dan.

Brooke stood in the doorway and smirked. Dan was crammed into the corner hunched over a computer. His muscular build looked silly in the small space. It was odd to see him out of uniform after all these years. With his promotion, he sported a white dress shirt with the sleeves rolled up exposing the ink up and down both arms. His man-bun was secured with a black hair tie.

"You might have to hide the tats before the Lieutenant sees them." Brooke warned.

Dan looked up, "I know... tell me something, do I look as ridiculously cramped as I feel?" He asked with a laugh.

"You've got to give it to the facilities guys, they somehow

30

squeezed another desk in here." Brooke said as she wiggled past Dan to her own desk and plopped her stuff down.

"Well get ready because if this is how close we are going to be at all times I hope your immune system is good. I have soon-to-be-four little ones who catch everything. When was the last time you had pink eye?" Dan said with a wink.

Brooke snorted. "Right. You keep your pink eyes and strep throats on that side of the office. Did June make coffee?" She fumbled around her desk, turning on her computer and pulling out her files from her bag.

"Was just brewing as I walked in, want me to grab you a cup? Just black or do you want something extra this morning to deal with your new partner?" Dan started to rise.

"I don't think I can pour Bailey's in my coffee and have no one notice." As Brooke said this Dan threw a crumbled-up paper ball at her. "I'll go and then let's go over the latest with the Blueberry Lane case. I think we can probably put it to bed today, then onto the call from yesterday I need to brief you on." Brooke started to get up to snake past Beal.

"Roger that." Dan gave her a miny salute as Brooke walked out.

* * *

Five minutes later, with coffee in hand Brooke and Dan went over the details of their first case as partners, which they had started when Dan was filling out the paperwork

31

for the promotion to detective. The case involved Jacey and Tim Trummel, a young couple with two small children. Jacey initially called 9-1-1 because Tim and she had a fight, which had led to him locking her out of the house. When Brooke and Dan had arrived, they found Jacey banging on the side door. Inside were two small children and Tim who was clearly intoxicated. They cited them both, instructed Tim to find another place to stay for the night or get taken to the station, and helped get Jacey an emergency protective order.

After reviewing their names in the database, Brooke and Dan found this was a pattern that happened quite often with these two. They seem to take turns calling the cops on each other and it wasn't long after this instance that Tim had called them back to Blueberry Lane because of Jacey.

"So, fill me in. What happened this weekend with our favorite lovebirds?" Brooke asked while sipping her coffee. *June really does make the best coffee,* Brooke thought.

"Jacey is currently being held at the county jail in Prince William." Beal waited for her reaction.

"Oh Lord. What did she do?" Brooke rolled her eyes.

"She was cited with public intoxication and...wait for it...assaulting an officer." Dan sat back in his chair.

"Really?" Brooke was shocked. In their dealings with Jacey, she had not been aggressive towards them. To Tim yes, but never an officer. Jacey had always been respectful and grateful when they showed up, regardless if it was her or Tim calling.

"Yep. From what I got through my contacts over there is that Tim was not with her, and no one can seem to find him." Dan was shifting through his handwritten notes now.

"You're about to tell me that the kids were with her aren't you." Brooke crossed her arms. She hated that those two young boys had witnessed so much violence between their parents.

Beal sighed. "They were. Apparently, that is where assaulting an officer comes in. They told her she either needed to call someone to come get the boys or they would call CPS. She shoved the arresting officer."

It was Brooke's turn to sigh now. "Where are they now?"

"Her mom came and got them. They are staying with her in Springfield while Jacey is being held. But CPS is involved, and I doubt they will allow her in the same house with the boys after what has transpired over the past two months." Dan shuffled his papers.

"Okay. So as far as FCPD is concerned I think we are out of this now. We responded to their calls, gave instructions on the protective order, which they both violated, and we called CPS as well." Brooke was going over her checklist out loud.

"Agreed. I can write it up and file it. I told the officer I know in Prince William to let me know who and I can send them our report and notes for their files too." Dan turned to face his computer.

"Perfect. Thanks Dan." Brooke was disheartened at how Jacey, and Tim for that matter, were parenting their boys.

Their shared office phone buzzed. It was June through the intercom. "Detective Hill, Detective Beal. I have a woman here wanting to speak to someone about a domestic violence situation. Her name is Catalina Dorado Hall. Could one of you come out and speak to her?"

Brooke and Dan looked at each other and nodded. Dan pressed the button down, "We will both be right out."

CHAPTER 6

As they walked towards the lobby Brooke briefly filled Dan in on the call from yesterday. "I told them to come in and we would look at what evidence they might have. I don't know that there will be anything here to even go with. Honestly, I am surprised they showed up." As Brooke was finishing her sentence June approached them with both Catalina and Maria at her side.

"Ah, here they are. This is Detective Brooke Hill and Detective Dan Beal. They are the lead detectives in our domestic violence unit." June said as an introduction. "Detectives, this is Catalina Dorado Hall and her Aunt Maria Alvarez."

"Thank you, June, it's nice to see you both." Brooke and Dan shook both women's hands. Catalina's look was downcast. She had yet to make eye contact with anyone. "June is conference room A available?" Brooke turned her attention to June as she asked.

"Yes, it is. I can unlock it for you all. Let me get the key." June grabbed the big golden key chain from her desk and the foursome followed her down the hall. Once in, they took their seats around the circular table. It was a small room with only four metal chairs around the table. Brooke looked at the wall which was haphazardly painted white over cinder blocks. The air smelled moldy, and Brooke wondered when the last time this room was used...or cleaned.

"I have the photos we talked about yesterday," Catalina's strongly accented voice was broken up with sobs.

"I am so sorry I know this is painful, but we need you to tell us everything about what brought you here today so we can take your official statement and then review the evidence you brought in." Brooke placed her hand on Catalina's.

"He took her *bebé! Él* . . . threatens her, *y*, uh, *tallos* her, *y ahora se ha llevado a su hijo.*" Catalina's Aunt Maria started yelling, her English morphing into more Spanish with each passing word. Neither Beal nor Brooke could understand the last bit. But Brooke understood the first half.

"Ma'am, I understand you are upset. We need to let Catalina tell us exactly what is going on and then we can proceed." Beal had turned his attention to the aunt to calm her down.

Catalina turned to her aunt and said something in Spanish and then continued in English turning towards Brooke. "My husband Matt and I met in college, American University. I got pregnant with our son Mateo during our senior year. We decided that I would put off law school and Matt would focus on providing for our family. After we had Mateo, Matt started working long hours and his excuses started not making sense. I called his office cell phone a few times and a woman picked up. When I questioned him, he hit me. That is when the abuse started. Before I knew it, I was being picked up by ICE agents and held in Farmville. I was there for a little over twenty-four hours. Matt posted bond, but when he came to get me, he told me he had moved my things out of our apartment, and I was not to see my son anymore. He took him to his parents who I can no longer get a hold of. I fled to my aunt's.....then the stalking started." Catalina paused to grab a tissue from the center of the table.

Beal was taking notes on a legal pad while Brooke and he listened intently. "I know you mentioned this yesterday and we didn't get into it, but what do you mean by stalking?" Brooke asked.

"Show her the pictures." Maria nudged Catalina.

Catalina reached into her bag and pulled out three photographs, two were in black and white and the third looked to be a photo from a cell phone. One was of a man banging on a front door, another of a man peering over a fence, and the third looked to be the same man crouched behind a car in a shopping center parking lot.

"I have been calling Matt to ask to see Mateo but haven't been able to get a hold of him. Then three nights ago he was banging on the front door of my aunt's house where I am staying, calling me all sorts of names. The next night at about two a.m. we saw him trying to get over the fence. These are screenshots from the security camera my Tia Maria has. We don't have a record video feature."

Brooke shook her head in acknowledgement. She knew that feature was pricey. "The third was from yesterday. I went to the food store by myself to pick a few things up. I looked over, and there he was. That's when my uncle convinced me to call the police" Catalina began to sob again.

"La poli," Maria spat in Brooke and Dan's direction.

"Do you have a picture of your husband that we could compare these images to?" Beal asked as he handed Catalina another tissue.

"Yes, I do." Catalina pulled out her cell phone and opened up the photo album. Beal and Brooke looked through about a half dozen photos date stamped from two and three months before all this. The images were grainy, but looked to be of the same person.

Brooke glanced at Dan and then turned back to Catalina. "Catalina, thank you for sharing this. I know reliving this is not easy. My partner and I are going to step out for a minute to discuss how best to proceed." Both Brooke and Dan stood up.

"Thank you," Catalina said as she grabbed another tissue.

"We will just be right in the hall." Brooke turned to walk out with Dan following her.

Once in the hall, they looked at each other. "What do you think?" Brooke asked her newly minted partner. He looked surprised that she would ask him to construct a possible plan first.

"He can't deny her parental rights, and she does seem scared so it's enough to warrant a temporary protective order. I don't know about the pictures and the ICE round-up though," Dan said as he peered into the conference room.

Brooke followed his gaze. The two women were huddled close together.

"I agree. I think a trip down to the courthouse to get her a temporary protective order and some resources is probably the best bet. And I agree with you: something is up with the ICE story and the stalking. I just don't know what." Brooke said.

"Do you believe her?" Dan asked pointedly.

"I don't know, something isn't adding up. I don't think she is telling us the whole story." Brooke sighed and looked into the conference room again. The two women were still huddled together, whispering.

"Listen, are you okay if I am the one who goes with them to the courthouse? I want to snoop around a bit there and see what I can find out about the ICE detainment. I also want my contact in the Commonwealth attorney's office to take a look at this." She didn't want to step on his toes, but she thought it might be better if she did this alone.

"I agree, and I was going to suggest it. I'm hoping she will be more comfortable because you are a woman, and you might be able to get more information out of her if I am not there. I'll stay behind and start the paperwork end." Dan smiled. "Ready?"

"Ready."

Dan twisted the doorknob to walk back into the conference room.

"Catalina, my partner, Detective Beal, and I think it is best if you go down to the courthouse. We think we have enough to get a temporary protective order. I'll go with you. While we're there, we can get you resources to get Mateo back." Brooke looked from Catalina to Aunt Maria.

"You aren't going to . . . arrest him?" Maria asked. She seemed annoyed that Brooke and Dan were not running out of there with their handcuffs in one hand and guns in the other.

"We don't have enough here to arrest him. We do have enough for a protective order and can get resources for Maria to get Mateo back into her custody." Beal directed his attention to the aunt as he answered in a calm voice.

The two women animatedly conversed in Spanish. Brooke and Dan looked at each other, before Dan leaned over to her and whispered, "I really wish I would have paid more attention in high school Spanish."

Brooke saw a hand go up out of the corner of her eye. "Thank you, detectives. We will do that now." Catalina interrupted her aunt as Maria was finishing her sentence in Spanish.

"I can go with you. Did you drive here?" Brooke asked.

"We Ubered," Catalina answered as her aunt crossed her arms and glared at both Brooke and Dan.

"I can take you in my car. Why don't you both wait out front, and I will be right there." Brooke reached for the door handle, but Dan beat her to it. It swung wide, and Brooke stepped out of the way to allow the two women ahead of her.

"Thank you, Detectives," Catalina said as she and her aunt walked out.

Brooke and Dan stared at each other, communicating on a level only two trained professionals who knew each other a long time can do. Dan went to say something out loud, but Brooke put her hand on his arm. "Beal, can you tell them I'll be right there? I need to make a phone call first."

She didn't wait for a response but pulled out her cell phone and walked down the hallway and out the side entrance of the precinct.

CHAPTER 7

After scurrying out of the police station into the fresh air, Brooke looked at her phone screen and tapped the contact she'd pulled up while pushing her way through the side door. She took a deep breath; the last time she had talked to Brian Keenan she was declining a dinner reservation because of Nick. She hadn't spoken to him in months, but she wanted an attorney's take on what Catalina had just told her, and Brian was the best the Commonwealth Attorney's Office had.

Brooke pressed her old college friend's name on her phone and listened to the ring. She needed him to pick up. She pushed her purple shirt sleeve up to her elbow as a way to fidget.

"Brooke hang on one second." Brian had picked up the phone on the second ring. She didn't have time to answer before she could hear muffled talking in the background. Before she knew it, he was back on again.

"Sorry about that, we have a new crop of interns in here for the semester, and the first few days are always chaotic. What's up? It's good to see your name flash across my phone." She could picture him now, propping his feet on his desk in his usual navy-blue suit, running his fingers over his dark walnut-colored hair, always cropped short. He had always been classically handsome.

"Hi Brian, I'm sorry it's been so long...and I am sorry that this isn't a more friendly call." Brooke looked up at the sky as she spoke. It was a beautiful day, one of those days where the sky is a clear beautiful blue color with perfect cotton-ball clouds sliding across the canvas.

"Figured it was too much to ask that you were calling after the past few months to reconsider my dinner invitation. How's it going with what's his name?"

Brooke could feel his smirk through the phone. She chuckled to acknowledge his ribbing.

"Nick is fine, although I doubt you were asking because you really care." Brooke knew she shouldn't flirt with Brian, but she couldn't help herself. She was still picturing him leaning back in his chair.

"Caught me. Okay what's up? What can I help with?" She heard a creak and had a sneaking suspicion that her mental picture had been correct, and he'd just sat up straight.

"I am actually headed to you in a few minutes with a domestic violence victim." Brooke again fumbled with her shirt as a way to deal with her nervous energy.

"You transport victims now?" Brian sounded surprised.

"Not normally a service I offer. She came into my station this morning." Brooke couldn't hide the hesitation in her voice.

"What's not sitting right with you?" Brian said, his voice now intent.

"I don't know. I can't put my finger on it." Brooke looked up at the sky again and sighed. Her gut was screaming, but she couldn't understand the language.

"Do you believe her?" Brian asked.

Brooke sighed again before answering. "There is definitely fear there."

"Then what is it?" Brian sounded confused.

"I don't know. I responded to a call yesterday and now she is here with her aunt who blew up at me and my partner when we said we would take her to the courthouse for a protective order and were not going to immediately arrest her husband." There was no way to hide her frustration. Her words came out quickly.

Brian let out a laugh. "So, they thought they could just walk into the police station, and you would turn around, run out, and arrest him."

Brooke chuckled at the ridiculousness as well. "Basically. I'm not sure if they know the way the law works though, the victim and her aunt are both immigrants. If it wasn't for an uncle in law enforcement, I don't think they would trust us to come forward."

"Tell me the details you can and that you know so far." Brian said in a very matter-of- business tone. All flirting and joking were over, and Brooke felt a pang of sadness, but she knew it was for the best.

"Victim's name is Catalina Dorado Hall. She is here with

her Aunt Maria-something. I don't have the notes right in front of me and can't remember the aunt's last name. Catalina says her husband Matt Hall became abusive after the birth of their first child, started cheating, pretty sure she thinks he called ICE on her, and is now stalking her. I responded last night to stalking claim, we took a report, and I told her to come in this morning with what evidence she has. She brought in pictures that she obtained from a video camera outside her aunt's house." Brooke took a deep breath waiting for Brian to say something. There was silence.

"Brian?"

"Brooke, do you know their child's name? Is it Mateo?" Brooke stood ramrod straight. *How did he know that?*

"Yes, they have a nineteen-month-old son named Mateo." Brooke was curious where Brian was going with this, *why would he ask this?*

"Brooke, I can't get involved. I know Matt. We went to high school together." Brian said it so matter-of-fact Brooke thought he might hang up on her.

"Brian I am not asking you to represent her or even give her legal advice for that matter. I just need another person who knows the system who can listen to her story. Help point her in the direction of some resources I may not have thought of." Brooke was annoyed by his quick reply.

"Brooke, no. I just pulled up his Instagram page right now. They are the picture-perfect family. His last post was just two weeks ago of the three of them and how lucky he is. I can't listen to her bash my high school friend." Brian was insistent he would not get involved.

But Brooke pressed on. "Brian please. Do you know how many Instagram picture perfect families I am called to for domestic violence? I am bringing her down to get a protective order. Your high school friend took her son from her and is not letting her see him. She has photos that look a lot like this friend of yours stalking her. When was the last time you even saw this guy? Is he actually a friend or are you using that term loosely?" Brooke knew she was being unkind but couldn't help it.

"That's not the point. I don't think I can objectively listen to this woman and not judge what she is saying about a person I've known for over fifteen years." Brian was now pleading with her.

"Brian, you are the only one I trust in your office. I know you will listen to her objectively and even though you don't believe yourself, I know you can be impartial. I am just asking you to meet with us when we get to the courthouse, listen to her, and tell me what you think. I know I am missing something, and it is driving me crazy." Brooke hoped that her last appeal worked.

Brian sighed. "What time will you be here? I am in and out of court today."

Yes! I got him, Brooke thought. "We can leave now and be there in about ten minutes if you will be free." Brooke crossed her fingers.

"I'm free till about 10:30." Brian sounded defeated.

"Perfect. That will give us a half hour once we get inside the courthouse." Brooke was starting towards the precinct door.

"Brooke, listen I will sit and meet with her and you to see if I pick up anything you might have missed. But I am telling you, I've known Matt for a long time. He wouldn't hurt anyone."

"Brian, I get it. I just need you to hear her out. For me." Brooke was grateful that even though he had valid misgivings he was willing to help her out.

"Man, Brooke, you owe me. I'll see you in a few."

CHAPTER 8

B ack inside the police station, feeling rejuvenated after negotiating with Brian, Brooke walked to the lobby and saw Catalina and her aunt deep in conversation. Maria was gesturing with her hands, and Brooke could tell she was still unhappy with their decision not to run out and arrest Matt.

Brooke approached the two women. "Catalina, Maria, thank you for waiting. I just need to pop into my office, then I will be right with you." Maria threw her hands up and spoke in rapid Spanish to Catalina.

Brooke waited. Finally, Catalina turned to face her.

"Thank you, Detective. It will just be me going to the courthouse. My Tia Maria needs to get back to work." Catalina turned to her aunt and said something in Spanish that made Maria go rigid and turn away.

Brooke nodded and walked down the hall to her office where Dan was busy doing paperwork at his desk. He turned as Brooke walked in. "Call it a hunch, but I am pretty sure the aunt isn't going to invite us over for dinner anytime soon."

Brooke laughed. "I don't know much Spanish, but I am

pretty sure the conversation I just overheard had nothing nice to say about us. I just got off the phone with my contact at the Commonwealth Attorney's Office."

"What'd they say?" Dan looked up at Brooke from his paperwork.

Brooke crossed her arms and looked at her partner. She wasn't used to sharing information with another person and debated for a second on how much to tell him. "Apparently he went to high school with Matt Hall and swears up and down that he would not hurt a fly."

"Really? What now? I can call over there and see if I can get someone down to meet with you?" Dan asked.

"No need. My contact, Brian Keenan, said he would meet us there and listen. I told him that something isn't sitting right and that I was not looking for legal advice. He's hesitant but is willing to do it even though he's worried about being biased." Brooke was trying to get her stuff together so she could get going, throwing what she could in her bag.

Dan was looking at her with a knowing smile. "What?" Brooke asked.

"Nothing." He was still smiling as he turned back to his computer.

"What do you know?" Brooke dropped her bag in the doorway.

"Nick may have mentioned something to me when you were in the will-they-won't-they stage." Dan couldn't hide his amusement. Brooke and Nick where in the will-they-won't-they stage of friendship for years before making it official.

Brooke rolled her eyes. "Goodbye Dan. I'll call you after."

"Tell Brian I said hi." Dan yelled as Brooke walked out their office door shaking her head. She pulled out her phone to check her messages before meeting Catalina. *Speak of the devil.* A text from Nick that she could not help but smile at and helped quiet her mind from the doubt earlier.

I love you Hill, never forget that.

* * *

Brooke and Catalina walked to Brooke's police issued black sedan that was parked in the back parking lot.

Catalina hesitated as they approached the sedan. "Everything okay?" Brooke stopped to turn towards her.

"Yea, sorry. I just never have been in a police car before. Do I sit in the back or the front?"

"Sorry it's procedure for you to sit in the back. Would you be more comfortable calling an Uber and I meet you there?" Brooke did not want to make Catalina uncomfortable.

"No. It's okay," Catalina got into the back of the sedan as Brooke held the door open.

Brooke had forgotten how awkward these car rides could be. She rarely escorts victims through this process personally, as a detective she normally doesn't get involved until officers have already responded to a domestic violence call or she's called in as back-up.

Brooke drove down the Fairfax County Parkway toward the courthouse, saying a silent prayer of thanks that the trip was short fifteen-minute ride. As Brooke turned her attention to the passing of cars and houses Catalina broke the silence.

"I'm sorry about my aunt. She is just really worried about me."

"I completely understand. You too are close?" Brooke looked in her rearview mirror back at Catalina.

"When my father was killed my mother took my sister Adriana and me to Maria's house here. It was a scary time, much like now." Catalina did meet Brooke's gaze and continued to watch the houses pass by.

"Are you close with your mom and sister?" Brooke was hoping that with the remaining few minutes in the car she could get some more information.

"Yes. My mother moved back to Colombia a few years ago to take care of my grandmother. Adriana lives in New York City now." Catalina remained staring out the window.

Brooke found an opening. "My sister lives in New York too. Is she acting? Going to school?" Brooke was counting on this newfound connection to help her uncover what she might be missing.

"She's going to school. NYU law. She wants to be an immigration attorney. We both do or did." Catalina turned to look at Brooke. "Do you think there is a chance they won't believe me? Whoever is in charge of protective orders?"

Brooke glanced back at her before turning her eyes back to the busy road. They were entering the government parking lot. Catalina concerned at the prospect of someone not believing her.

"I don't think you need to worry about that. Unless you're a good actress, you can't fake the fear you seem to be experiencing, and a judge will see that. The courthouse will have offices and resources to help you navigate everything you are going through."

"I hope you are right." Catalina turned again to face the window.

As she pulled into the parking garage and got out of the car Brooke checked her phone. There was one text waiting to be read from her fiery redhead best friend Jacs. The two of them have been inseparable since second grade.

Brooke smiled at the words on her screen, a welcome reprieve from the drama unfolding in her day. *The Hill is killing me today! (Not you, Congress :)) Freddie's tonight? First rounds on me. You can bring your stupid boyfriend too :).*

Jacs worked for the Armed Services Committee in the Senate, and while Brooke didn't always fully understand what she did on any given day, she knew it was stressful, and Freddie's was their place to let off steam.

Their favorite bar just so happened to be the best drag bar in Northern Virginia.

Brooke made a mental note to text Jacs back and Nick. She smiled at the thought of spending the night with two of her favorite people, they always had a good time together at Freddie's.

Brooke turned to Catalina as they got out of the car. "I called one of the Commonwealth Attorneys I know. He is going to meet us inside the courthouse and help navigate all this." Brooke pulled out her phone to call Brian as they began walking towards the stairs that lead to the double front doors.

"You here?" His voice was clipped. *What was with him not saying hello on the phone anymore?*

"We are walking up now." Brooke said as she walked up the hill towards the front doors of the courthouse.

"I'll meet you at the info desk just past the metal detectors." With those instructions, Brian hung up. *So much for saying goodbye either.*

As she and Catalina walked through the doors, Brooke said a silent prayer hoping Brian could help Brooke see the missing piece.

CHAPTER 9

Brooke spotted Brian as soon as she and Catalina were through the metal detectors. He was leaning against the information desk talking to one of the volunteers. Brian turned and a smile spread across his face. *I forgot how handsome he is.* Brooke caught herself before almost saying the words out loud.

Brian approached Catalina and Brooke. "Detective Hill," he stuck out his hand to shake hers. Brooke knew the formality was for Catalina's sake. "And you must be Mrs. Hall," Brian turned to Catalina to shake her hand. "Nice to meet you, I'm Brian Keenan. I'm from the Office of the Commonwealth Attorney. I reserved the conference room right up this hallway for us to chat." He pointed towards the right and the two women fell in step behind him as they followed him across the shiny, white-tiled flooring. Brooke's heels clacked on the surface, making her look at Catalina's shoes to compare since no sound came from the shorter woman in front of her. Catalina's sneakers were white with dirt stains and obvious wear on the toe boxes.

"Right here," Brian gestured to an open door and led

the way in. The conference room resembled the one at the station Catalina and Brooke were just in with a small wood table and four matching office chairs. The three of them sat at the round conference table and Brian began.

"Mrs. Hall, Detective Hill briefed me on what you shared with her at the station. I know this is hard, but I would like you to share with me what you told Detective Hill." Brooke was struck by Brian's professionalism, considering he was so worried about being objective.

"Is that really necessary? I just spoke to Detective Hill about all this an hour ago, and you just said she shared with you what I said." Brooke detected a hint of annoyance in Catalina's voice that had not been there before. Was she tired of retelling her story already, or was it something else? Did she recognize Brian as a friend of her husband's?

Brian looked at Brooke for help and she jumped in. "I'm sorry, Catalina, but yes. You will, unfortunately, have to retell this story several times—just today even." Brooke put her hand over Catalina's. "I promise it will get easier the more often you tell it."

Catalina muttered a phrase in Spanish. Brian raised one eyebrow at Brooke. Then the Spanish turned to English. "My husband Matt and I have been married for two years now. We have a son Mateo who is nineteen-months. Matt got abusive shortly after our son was born. He began working long hours . . . and I believe he was sleeping with someone. I questioned him about this, and the next thing I knew, ICE was at my door. I was held for twenty-four hours. Matt posted bail, but when we went to go home, he told me he'd taken our son to his parents, and I had no place to go. He'd even ordered me an Uber instead of driving me away from the detention center. Then, after I moved into my aunt's house, the stalking began." Catalina had not started to sob during this retelling like she had before. Instead, she was stoic.

As Brooke listened to Catalina's story, something seemed out of order. Brooke tried to recall the events when Catalina had first told both her and Dan of her situation.

"Can you describe the stalking?" Brian was listening intently. Catalina pulled out the photos she had shown Brooke earlier as she explained what she'd experienced.

Brooke wracked her brain. *Okay, first the baby, then long hours, then abuse started after she accused him of cheating—that's it!*

Catalina had finished talking, pulling Brooke to the present. Brian was holding the photos. "Thank you for sharing these with me." He handed them back to her. "Detective Hill, do you have anything to add?" Brian and Catalina looked at Brooke.

"Just one thing. Catalina, when we spoke this morning, you said the abuse started after you called your husband and a woman picked up the phone." Brooke turned her chair to face Catalina. She hoped she wasn't coming off accusatory. She didn't want Catalina to feel like she was under attack.

"Yes, it did." Catalina seemed genuinely confused.

"Just now, speaking with Mr. Keenan, you stated the abuse started right after your son was born." Catalina's eyes grew wide, and her mouth opened, then closed, but no sound came out.

After a half-minute, she asked, "Does it matter? There was abuse. Isn't that enough? This is a very stressful and scary time. I would think what matters is that abuse happened." Catalina was not yelling, but her tone was defensive, and her eyes filled with tears.

Brian jumped in before Brooke could reply. "Yes, of course. However, you will be appearing before a judge to petition the court for a protective order. You need to have the facts straight. And true. You can't have two different accounts of when the abuse started." It was Brian's turn to sound annoyed, if not a touch accusatory.

So much for trying to be objective, Brooke thought.

Catalina stared blankly from one to the other.

"Catalina, when did the abuse start?" Brian asked point blank.

"After I confronted my husband about sleeping with someone else. I misspoke earlier." Catalina lowered her gaze to her lap.

"Okay. The next step is to file a petition for a protective order through the Juvenile and Domestic Relations Court. I had one of my clerks start to fill out the paperwork for you after I spoke to Detective Hill. I just need you to verify everything and sign here." Brian handed the form to Catalina with a pen, which he pointed to the line at the bottom.

As Catalina signed, Brooke and Brian exchanged looks. It was a knowing look, but what exactly they knew after this exchange neither of them could be sure.

"I will walk you and Detective Hill upstairs to the offices. One of the representatives from the Juvenile and Domestic Relations Office is waiting up there for us. They will walk you through what to expect regarding the protective order, as well as give you additional resources through the county to help you navigate everything." Brian stood up and approached the door.

"They will help me get my son back?" Catalina asked as she looked up at Brian and then to Brooke. She had remained seated as they both stood.

"They will point you to resources, yes." Brian opened the door. "It is just one floor up on the escalator." Brian motioned for Brooke and Catalina to follow him out of the conference room, toward the escalators.

Once on the second floor, Brooke touched Catalina's arm to prompt her to turn around. "I can't walk you into the office. The meeting with the representative will just be you and him. I can wait here for you and then wait till they call you into court. Once we file the petition for the protective order, it won't be long before they will call you before the judge."

"Thank you for everything, Detective Hill. It's just through here?" Catalina gestured to the glass double doors in front of them.

"Yes. I believe you are meeting with Chris Michaels, so ask for him." Brian moved to escort Catalina through the doors but then stopped and turned. "Detective Hill, I will just be a minute. Can you wait here for me?"

Brooke nodded and watched the two of them disappear through the double doors. Brian's poker face was good. She knew he'd been annoyed with Catalina's answers, but she couldn't read how he was feeling about this case overall.

Brooke felt her cell phone vibrate in her pants pocket. She pulled it out to see a message from Nick. *Jacs just texted me and told me Freddie's tonight. Actually, she said you and her were going and she guessed I could come. Sorry for being so distracted this morning. I'll meet you there after your shift. Love you.*

Meet you there. Love you. Brooke didn't want to say any more than that for fear of giving away her insecurities about the morning. As she put her phone back in her pocket, Brian reappeared through the double doors.

"You're right. Something's not quite right with the story we were just told."

CHAPTER 10

B rooke took a deep breath in. She had mixed feelings about Brian confirming her suspicions that Catalina's story had holes, and she might be hiding something.

"What do you think it is?" Brooke asked.

"I don't know. Something isn't adding up." Brian crossed his arms and leaned against the wall. Brooke was standing so close to him she could smell his cologne; the scent of sandalwood filled her nose. He loosened his tie and rolled his neck.

"Talk me through what you are thinking, because like I said before, I can't put my finger on it." Brooke matched Brian's body language and crossed her arms while leaning on the wall no more than a foot from him. She could feel the heat from his body compared to the cold corridor.

"It's not just the discrepancy in timeline about when the abuse started. That isn't enough for me to doubt her. But there's something in my gut needling me."

"Exactly. . .. But . . . Look, Brooke, I am trying not to be biased. I really am. And I hate to say I don't believe a victim of abuse . . ." Brian sighed and looked at the ceiling.

"So, you *don't* believe her?" Brooke raised her eyebrows.

She could agree that something wasn't adding up, but there was real fear there. Brooke was sure of that, *wasn't she?*

Brian slowly shook his head. "I don't. It's not just that I know Matt, either." He turned his attention from the ceiling to Brooke, looking into her eyes with compassion.

Brooke couldn't help it. Despite his empathy, she felt annoyed. "Okay, then what is it?"

"It is her whole demeanor. The abuse is awful, but there were no specifics. And stalking can be just as bad, but this woman was *just* detained by ICE and had her son taken away by her now-estranged husband. I feel like she put barely any emphasis on either of those things. They were just passing statements. If I had a son, that would be my first priority. Don't you agree?" Brian leaned forward a little, and Brooke inhaled more of his cologne, making her insides flutter. She backed up.

"I agree—somewhat. I think her demeanor is part of what is throwing me off, yes. I told you her aunt was pissed off that we weren't running out of the station with guns blazing to go arrest him . . ."

"There is a 'but' in there, where you are going to disagree with me?" Brian asked with a smirk.

Brooke smiled, her frustration dissipating with Brian's banter. "There is. She didn't go into detail about the ICE detainment, but that is not why she came to see me—us. Who am I to judge how a mother acts when they can't see their child, especially such a young child? Catalina spoke several times, with and without tears, about needing to be with her son. It felt like a priority earlier. I don't know her other than what I've witnessed today and yesterday, so who's to say being calm—especially more so than her aunt—isn't just her personality?" Brooke softened her tone as she spoke.

Brian rolled his neck again and looked back up at the ceiling. "How can I help?" When he looked back at Brooke, waiting for an answer, his eyes conveyed a deep friendship, which Brooke knew had been rattled when she'd turned him down for the dinner invitation. It made her nearly speechless. "What?"

"Are you honestly going to tell me you aren't going to look into this further? Just help her get a temporary protective order and walk away?" Brian raised one eyebrow.

He was right. "You have me all figured out, huh?" Brooke smiled.

"Well, it helps having known you for over ten years." Brian matched her grin, and a shallow dimple emerged in his left cheek. It doesn't appear often, but when it did, it was endearing. "Just don't make me regret asking how I can help you."

Brooke raised her eyebrows. "Deal. . ... So how well do you know Matt Hall?"

Brian let out a little laugh, acknowledging that Brooke was hinting at something. "I knew his brother better, Andrew. Matt was a year younger than me. I saw Andrew not that long ago. We were all on the baseball team together."

"Feel like reaching out to your old high school buddy?

You know, catch up, have a drink maybe? Talk?" Brooke said as she closed the gap between them and nudged his side with her elbow. He uncrossed his arms to block the move. Brooke couldn't tell if it was a reflex or if she'd gone too far.

"I could do that. However, you have to understand that anything we discuss that I don't feel is necessary for you to know, I'm not sharing." Brian said, recrossing his arms.

"Okay, fair." Brooke nodded.

"What are you going to do?" Brian asked.

"I'm going to look more into this ICE detainment. She might not be a citizen, but she is married to an American citizen, her son is one and has never been in trouble...not even a speeding ticket. Something isn't right. Why pick her up?" Brooke asked.

"Agreed." Brian nodded. "I have a contact who is pretty high up in the DC central office. I'll text it to you when I get back to my office."

"Thank you, Brian. I really appreciate it. I know this is not something you wanted to get involved in. . . . And I know you are doing this for me—for our friendship. I know I've been distant since, well, you know." Brooke reached out and touched his arm.

"You owe me, Brookie." Brian winked. "Don't you have a partner now who can be doing this with you?"

Brooke laughed. "Yeah, but he's not childhood buddies with our alleged offender."

The double doors opened, and Catalina walked out with

a pile of papers. She approached them looking flustered. "Thank you. I met with Chris. He put me in touch with legal aid and CPS. I now have to wait to be called in to see the judge for the protective order."

Brian stood up straight, tearing himself off the wall. "I am glad we could help. Detective Hill, I need to head back to my office. I will text you that number and let you know about the other thing too." Brian turned and strode down the hallway.

Brooke saw a questioning look on Catalina's face. Before the woman had a chance to ask Brooke anything, the court officer announced, "Catalina Dorado Hall."

The woman took a deep breath, and Brooke said, "I'll be right here waiting when you are finished."

"Thank you, Chris prepped me as well. He told me to act scared." Catalina took a second deep breath and walked toward the large oak courtroom doors.

Act scared? Brooke thought. It was Brooke's turn to take a deep breath. There was definitely something up with Catalina Dorado Hall and her story.

CHAPTER 11

"**D**id they grant her one?" Jacs took a sip of her lemon drop martini as she asked Brooke about the protective order drama Brooke had just unloaded on her. They were perched at their usual red linoleum bar-top table at Freddie's Gay Bar, and Violet, their favorite drag queen, was serving them their drinks. Tonight's theme was "disco divas," and Violet did not disappoint. Dressed in head-to-toe purple as a nod to her name, she had outdone her typically outlandish fashion choices. Highlighted by flared pants and a long-sleeved top with sparkles, the outfit had been completed with a purple rhinestone belt and glasses to match. Her usual purple wig was replaced with a black afro one.

"Another round for my favs?" Violet leaned over the bar, exposing a stuffed, black-laced bra.

A "No" and a "yes" were heard in unison from Brooke and Jacs, respectively, as they argued about having another round.

"It's been a long day, and Nick hasn't even shown up yet!" Jacs reached out to Violet's hand. "Yes, Violet dear, another round, and can I just say you look exceptional tonight. I wish I could do my makeup like you."

"I'll teach ya," Violet said with a wink. "Same drinks or are we changing them up?"

"Same thing," Brooke said quickly, practically choking on her vodka soda. She wanted to speak up before Jacs had the chance to order her go to cure for a bad day: tequila shots.

Jacs frowned. "Okay, so did they?"

"Did they what?" Brooke was genuinely confused. "Oh, protective order! Yes. She got one. Temporary. She walked out of court very happy." Brooke's tone changed. Even she heard it.

"You don't like that she was happy?" Jacs seemed confused.

"It's not that. It's just that it seemed more like a celebration than a relief." Brooke took another sip of her drink.

"Hey, sorry I'm late." Nick had walked up behind them without Brooke noticing. He kissed her on the cheek and gave a side hug to Jacs. He was dressed in his usual off-duty fit: wranglers and a white T-shirt.

"How far behind am I?" He grabbed the stool next to Brooke.

"Not far at all, hon. Want your usual?" Violet had appeared with more drinks.

"V, you look amazing tonight, as always. And yes please." Nick leaned forward in his stool toward Violet.

"Good-looking and good manners. When she's done with you, you let me know." Violet turned to get Nick his beer. Everyone laughed except Brooke.

"Sorry I'm late. I got caught up in something. What did I miss?" Nick grabbed the beer from Violet.

Got caught up in something? With what? With who? Brooke tried to shake it off but caught Jacs's glance at her.

"Brooke was just catching me up on her case from today," Jacs said while finishing her first drink and grabbing her second.

"New case?" Nick turned to Brooke with a raised eyebrow. "By the way, Jacs, casual day at work?" Nick was laughing as he said this. Jacs normal business wear was met tonight with sweats and her beautiful red hair in a ponytail.

"Listen, Simons, don't start with me. I had senators yelling at me all morning, and I took a half-day." Jacs leaned in, pointing her perfectly red polished finger into Nick's chest.

Nick raised both hands in surrender and turned to Brooke, apparently waiting for her to tell him about her latest case.

She obliged. "It's not really a case, at least not yet. It's the call from yesterday. The woman came into the station and sought help with a domestic violence situation. I escorted her to court for the temporary protective order. It's just something about the whole story isn't sitting right with me." Brooke looked at Nick. She realized this is the first time their eyes have met since before the phone call this morning.

"Go with your gut. It hasn't failed you yet. Don't worry; you will get to the bottom of it—like always." Nick turned his eyes to the overhead TV. There was something about the way he'd said it. It was almost cold, sarcastic, not how he normally spoke to her, even before they'd started dating. Brooke again tried to shake it off and noticed Jacs giving her the side eye again.

"What's the latest with air mattress?" Nick asked before taking a sip of his beer. Jacs and Brooke had a habit of nicknaming anyone they dated. Jacs's latest boy-toy didn't have an actual bed, just an air mattress. Having Nick ask about him using his nickname made Brooke giggle, and Jacs glared at Brooke for spilling her secret.

As Jacs was summarizing their latest date and the awkward way he ate sushi— "with a spoon guys! A spoon!"— Nick's phone rang. He looked down and silenced it quickly.

Don't overthink it. Brooke told herself. But Nick's phone began to ring again.

He sighed heavily. "Sorry guys, I have to take this." He got up and walked out of sight before either of them could say anything.

Brooke's gaze followed him out. When she turned around, Jacs was staring at her. "Do you want to talk about it?" her best friend asked sympathetically.

"I don't know if there is anything to talk about at this point." Brooke stared into her drink as she spoke.

"The eff there isn't. Something is up with the two of you." Jacs tapped the table in front of Brooke, forcing her to look up.

"Nick got a call like this early this morning, and ever since, I don't know, things have been off. And yes, I asked about it. He brushed it off, said something about his dad. And then June . . ." Brooke took a sip of her drink. Jacs gave her a look and gestured with her hand to keep talking. "June stopped me this morning and said Nick was getting calls at the station this morning too. I don't know, Jacs. Something doesn't feel right." Brooke could feel her throat constricting with emotion.

"And?" Jacs asked.

"And . . . all the things. Because I am doubting what is going on with Nick, I am doubting everything, including this latest 'case.'" She made quotation marks with her fingers. "You and I both know Nick doesn't exactly have the best track record with relationships, and I know, I know . . . you are going to say he would never do anything to mess this up." Brooke looked down at her drink again.

"I'm not going to say that at all. I fully expect him to mess this up," Jacs admitted, finishing her second martini before trying to get Violet's attention.

"Wait, what?" Brooke was shocked. Jacs had been advocating for Nick and Brooke to get together for years.

"Brooke, it's Nick. He is bound to make a mess of this. But you love him, and he loves you." Jacs shrugged. "I'm not trying to brush you off, so stop looking at me like that." Jacs sighed and began again. "Look, he is definitely hiding something, and if it is something that will hurt you, I will kill him. But you need to decide. Do you trust what he is telling you, or do you not?"

"What do I do if I don't trust what he says?" Brooke asked.

"You have two options: you either question him to death till it leads to a big fight, and he tells you during a screaming match. Or you suffer in silence. But decide quickly because he just walked back in."

Brooke turned as Nick sat down. He didn't just look stressed; he looked sad too.

"Are you okay?" Brooke and Jacs asked in unison.

"Fine, just a lot going on at the moment," Nick said, running his fingers through his hair.

"Pretty sure that is a lyric to a Taylor Swift song." Jacs turned her attention to the bar.

"I know I just got here, but I'm exhausted. Brooke, you okay if I head out? I'm going to go home and get some sleep. I was never able to fall back to sleep this morning." Nick touched Brooke's arm.

"Oh, okay. You're going home to your home or mine?" Brooke asked, looking up at him. She was still seated on the bar stool, not wanting to move for fear of falling down in an emotional heap.

"I'm going to go to my place, I think," Nick said, motioning to Violet.

"Hey, V, can you run my card? I'll pick up the tab for these two as well," he said with a wink.

He can flirt with our drag queen waitress but not with me, his alleged girlfriend, Brooke thought as she finished her drink.

"Brooke? Did you hear me? Did you drive?"

Brooke was lost in her thoughts and didn't hear Nick at first. She shook her head to bring herself back to the present. "Sorry, no Jacs picked me up."

"Jacs, you okay if I steal Brooke and take her home?" Nick said, looking at Jacs.

Jacs looked from Brooke to Nick. "Yeah, I have to head home now, anyway—early morning."

Brooke hugged Jacs. "Only you can decide how you handle this situation. Not him," Jacs whispered in Brooke's ear.

Brooke squeezed Jacs a little harder. "I know." Then she turned and followed Nick out.

CHAPTER 12

Brooke followed Nick to his truck, hoping that him wanting to drive her home early was because he wanted to talk. He opened the passenger door and, before she stepped up, he kissed her softly. "I love you," he whispered in her ear.

Brooke allowed herself to relax to enjoy the fleeting intimacy. "I love you too." Brooke searched his eyes, looking for some reassurance. "Look, I know something is going on. If you aren't ready to talk about it, will you promise me you will soon?"

"I will. I'm just not ready yet." He kissed her again before she could say anything else and helped her up and into the truck.

They didn't speak during the twenty minutes it took to get her home. Brooke felt like crying, the space and distance between them feeling enormous.

As Nick pulled into her driveway, she turned to him. "You sure you don't want to sleep here?"

"I need a goodnight's sleep in my own bed. Tomorrow?" He looked exhausted, almost beaten down. His eyes darkened from the big bags under them.

Brooke couldn't help it, a tear started down her cheek. She quickly wiped it away. Nick was staring straight ahead at her house, avoiding eye contact.

"Nick." Brooke's voice was shaky. After the day, the secrecy, and the drinks, there was no hiding that she knew he was keeping something big from her. "I know something is—" Brooke didn't get to finish her sentence.

"I can't talk about this yet," Nick said, turning toward her. There was something different about the way he looked at her then. The love behind his eyes that she had experienced for years, both in friendship and now in love, seemed to be gone. *Hidden.*

"What could be so bad that after all these years, both as friends and more, that you can't talk to me about it?" Brooke was pleading.

Nick let a long sigh out. "Can you please just respect the fact that I am not ready to discuss this with you yet?" Again, he avoided looking at her.

"Nick," Brooke pulled his face toward hers. "You need to let me help you. When we moved past friends, we became a team. Please, let me help you."

"Brooke—" Nick started.

"Please, Nick, please don't say you can't talk about it right now. Please let me help you." Brooke said a silent prayer that she was getting through to him.

Nick drummed the steering wheel with his thumbs. "Why can't you just let things be?"

Shock coursed through her, making her heart race. Quite suddenly, Nick seemed annoyed. Angry even.

"Excuse me?"

"Look, Brooke, I get you are worried, but I have told you several times that I'm not ready to talk about what's going on. You have to let me have some space to process things, and then we can talk about it." He ran his fingers through his hair, this time with frustration, making part of it stand up on his head.

"Seriously?" The tears had stopped. It was now her turn to be frustrated. "I am more than worried. You are scaring me."

"Scaring you? Don't you think you are being a little dramatic?" Nick said with an undertone of cruelty.

Brooke couldn't believe what was happening. She and Nick had never, in all their years of friendship, ever communicated to each other like this.

Guess I am going with Jacs' option one, Brooke thought before speaking. "Actually, no, not at all. In fact, I think I have kept it together well today. You become increasingly secretive about calls, seem worried after each one, and you aren't yourself."

"I'm stressed. I'm allowed to be stressed." Nick said, turning away to stare out his driver's side window.

"I didn't say you weren't, but you have to understand that your behavior after getting these calls is concerning. As your girlfriend, I am allowed to be concerned." Brooke reached out to touch Nick's forearm. He flinched.

"I'm acting normal." Nick looked at her. Even in the moonlight, she could see the stress lines wipe themselves across his face like a napkin as he clinched his jaw.

77

"There is no way you actually believe that." Brooke tried to soften her expression.

"Jesus, Brooke, please just leave it alone!" His voice seemed to echo inside the cab. Brooke couldn't remember a time ever hearing Nick raise his voice like that. The tears welled in her eyes. She tried to hold them back but couldn't. She couldn't help her reaction to the way he had just spoken to her. She covered her face with her hands.

"Please don't cry, Brooke." Nick instantly softened and pulled her hands into his. "I'm sorry. I didn't mean to react the way I just did. It has been a lot today, and I am not ready to talk about it yet. I just really need you to understand that."

"We went from telling each other everything to keeping secrets in an instant. I don't know how to just be okay with this." Tears streamed down Brooke's cheeks. Nick attempted to wipe them away with his hand, but she leaned away from him.

"I'm not keeping secrets. I'm just not ready to talk about it. To discuss it." He was beginning to sound more like himself, but Brooke wasn't satisfied with this answer.

"But you are so not acting like yourself, and I am not the only one who has noticed. How am I not supposed to be concerned? I have to ask, is this thing that you aren't ready to talk about going to hurt me? Hurt us? Please, Nick, I need answers." More tears started down her cheeks.

"Jacs doesn't count. She's going to agree with you because she is your best friend. Of course she is going to say something is up, and I am not acting normal because that is what you believe." Nick once again faced forward.

"It's not just her. June—"

"June what?" Nick cut Brooke off and turned to face her. Annoyance once again evident in his eyes as they narrowed.

Brooke hesitated for a moment. She wasn't sure how much she should tell him, given that reaction. "Well, June didn't say anything about how you were acting, but she did say it was weird that you were getting early morning calls at the station."

"She shouldn't have told you that." Nick rolled down his window, presumably to get some air.

"Don't be mad at her. June only said something to me because she was concerned." Brooke thought about reaching out to him again but didn't. She didn't want him to flinch. That reaction had hurt too much the first time. She didn't think she could handle it again.

"We aren't getting anywhere." Nick turned toward her. He put her head in his hands. "I love you—I really do. I need you to trust me and know that I will talk to you about this, just not right now."

Brooke took a deep breath. It didn't go unnoticed that he never answered if whatever he was keeping was going to hurt her or their relationship. "I love you too," she managed to whisper.

"Let's both get some sleep. I'll call you in the morning." Nick unlocked the doors.

Guess that's my cue. She got out of the car.

Brooke shuffled up her driveway and turned into the carport to wave, but Nick was already pulling out the driveway—too busy to notice her.

CHAPTER 13

"Where's Mommy?"

It's so hot . . . so bright.

There's a strong hand on her shoulder.

"I want my Mommy!"

Wetness . . . oh, the tears.

* * *

Brooke woke up to her face drenched and her heart racing. Staring up at her mini chandelier on her bedroom ceiling, she took a few deep breaths. *It was just a dream*, she kept repeating herself. She reached out for Nick. Her heart sank as the weight of the last twenty-four hours came crashing back.

Brooke could feel her adrenaline start to ease, but she still felt like she needed some comfort, some help. Brooke put her glasses on and grabbed her phone to see what time it was. *A little after two—I can still get about three hours before having to wake up*, Brooke thought.

She walked barefoot into her kitchen to make a cup of tea. Aunt T had gifted her an instant water boiler she'd found on Amazon last Christmas. Brooke said a silent prayer, thanking her aunt. It had been a lifesaver in many similar moments.

Armed with her chamomile tea, Brooke shuffled back into her bedroom to look for her purple shag weighted blanket. *Tea, blanket, and a little* Bewitched *should do the trick.* Watching Bewitched had always been comforting to Brooke. She could vividly remember cuddling on the couch in her childhood home, watching reruns with her mom, who always hummed the theme song.

Brooke propped herself up on her pillows and adjusted her blanket. She picked one of her favorite episodes, the one where Tabitha was born. As the theme song began to play through her TV, her eyes felt suddenly heavy. Placing her tea on the nightstand, she snuggled under the blanket. She was sound asleep before the opening scene.

* * *

Brooke sat straight up, waking up startled. An infomercial was playing loudly on her TV. She reached for the remote and turned off the gentleman who was selling knives. Then she looked at her phone. It read 4:55 a.m., five minutes before her alarm was supposed to go off. *Ugh.* She hated when this happened.

Under the time was a new message, from Nick. Brooke grabbed her glasses and typed her password to open her phone. He'd sent it about an hour ago.

I can't sleep. I hate the way we left things. I hate that you are worried. I hate that you are scared. I hate that I caused this, and worst of all, I hate that I made you cry. I love you. I never want to hurt you. I just need to process what is going on and then we can talk. There was a lot of information today—I am just trying to sort through it. I hope you can understand that. It's a me thing not a you thing, even though I know my actions affect you. I love you Hill. Please forgive me for the way I have been acting. I am the dramatic one, not you. Please call me when you wake up. I am sure I will still be up.

Brooke didn't even think. She picked up the phone and tapped on his name.

He picked up after just one ring. "I'm so sorry. I understand if you don't want to talk to me after the way I spoke to you. You don't deserve that. I am so sorry, Brooke." He sounded awful. A mixture of exhaustion and desperation came through in his voice.

"Nick—" Brooke started.

"Did I mention how sorry I am? And that I love you. And that you are beautiful." Nick interrupted. Brooke couldn't help it, she let out a giggle, born from relief.

"My intention was not to fight, Nick," Brooke's voice was soft, both from sleep and purposefully trying to soften the situation.

"I know. And my reaction was because of stress, not because of you. I 100 percent understand that the way I act affects you . . . and that is because you care. Which

I am so grateful for. I hope you know I would never intentionally do anything to blow it with you. I waited years for this to happen. To be with you this way." Nick was sounding more and more like the old Nick.

"I know," Brooke said softly.

"I get that this is asking a lot, but can you please trust me on this? Yes, it is something that has me stressed, but I need to process it by myself, before I talk to you about it. And you will be the first person I talk to. I'm just not ready yet." Nick's voice took on a pleading tone again.

Jacs's voice ran out in Brooke's head: *"You need to decide: Do you trust what he is telling you or do you not?"*

Brooke let out a long breath. "Okay."

"Okay?" Nick asked.

"Okay. I trust you, Nick. I trust that whatever has you so worried, we can work it out. I trust that this isn't you-not-trusting-me issue but a you-need-to-process-this-first thing. I hope you can understand that this is just difficult to navigate with how you were acting yesterday." Brooke took off her glasses and wiped her eyes of the sleepiness.

"Thank you. I love you." Nick sounded relieved.

"I love you too." Brooke pulled her weighted blanket up closer to her neck.

"I didn't sleep at all last night. I'm going to knock off for a few hours before I have to go in. I'll stop by your office when I get there. I really do love you," Nick said again.

"Ditto, Simons. I'll see you later." Brooke tapped the

disconnect button and placed her phone face-down on the bed. She felt relieved that they had spoken, and Nick seemed more like himself than he had yesterday. While that was comforting, she couldn't help but be upset by him keeping whatever was bothering him to himself. "You just have to trust him," Brooke coached herself.

Brooke was contemplating who Nick's mystery caller could be when her phone rang. It was Brian. "Good morning, Detective Hill." She could hear his smile through the phone.

"You know what time it is, right?" Brooke laughed.

"Unfortunately, yes. I am getting up for a run and figured you were up and moving for work. Are you busy?" Brian asked.

"Just busy putting off getting ready. What's up?" Brooke sat on the edge of her bed and looked for her slippers. Her engineered hardwood floors were cold first thing in the morning, no matter what time of year it was.

"I met my old childhood buddy, Drew Hall, last night for a drink." Brooke could tell that Brian knew she would be surprised and was waiting for her reaction.

"That was quick." Brooke had stopped searching and was sitting on her knees on her bed.

"I was surprised, too. But I reached out after I left you. He wanted to make plans right away. I was thinking if you had time, I could stop by the station on my way to the courthouse. Are you free around eight or eight-thirty?" Brian asked.

"I should be. Get anything good from him?" Brooke had started to stand up.

"Let's just say it's *interesting*."

CHAPTER 14

Brooke tried in vain to stay focused while her mind whirled and skipped from one topic to the next as she drove to the station. *If everything is okay with Nick and me, why do I feel this way? What did Brian find out? Is it really his dad who is stressing Nick out so much? I wonder if Beal is in yet. I really could use Starbucks.* Her head was spinning.

The sound of her cell phone ringing brought her back to the present. She answered without looking at the caller ID.

"Hey, kid." The familiar, rich voice of Benji Noble filled her car's Bluetooth. Benji wasn't just the former lead detective for the domestic violence unit or her mentor, he was so much more. Benji and his wife Carol were Brooke's adoptive family. Since teaching her in the academy and introducing himself as the police officer who had rescued her and her sister Cassie the night her parents perished in the fire, he had been an instrumental part of her life. Sunday dinners and shared holidays were a regular occurrence between the Nobles and Brooke, Cassie, and Aunt T.

"Benji—hi!" Brooke was genuinely surprised any time he called or texted. Random pop-ins at the station were normally his thing. At first, she'd felt like he was checking up on her in his former role, but she soon realized he wouldn't have recommended her if he thought she wasn't capable. He was just a nice guy, looking to reconnect with the police force he had called his family.

"Hi, sweetheart!" The unmistakably sweet Southern voice of Carol came through the speaker too. By the sound of her "Deep Peach" accent, you would think she'd just left Georgia a week ago, not forty years now.

"Carol, hi! Wow, I get both Nobles before 8:00 a.m. What do I owe the pleasure?" Just hearing their voices calmed the racing thoughts in Brooke's head and the pounding of her heart in her chest.

"I shaved off my mustache, and we are moving to Bali!" Benji let out a laugh. Benji had become much more lighthearted since retiring six months ago. Brooke now understood all too well the stress of the job.

"Right. You've had that mustache practically since birth, even if it has changed from brown to—what would you call that, Benji, white or gray?" Brooke had learned to give it right back to Benji in their humor sparring matches.

"I like to think of it as silver." Brooke could picture Benji driving their navy Volvo SUV and turning to Carol and smiling.

"I'm going to interrupt before he starts referring to himself as a silver fox," Carol said with a laugh. "Brooke, are you and Nick free for dinner tonight? I sent Benji to the store last night to pick up pizza dough to make calzones, and he bought too much of everything. So, we are making homemade pizzas tonight."

"That sounds great. I'll definitely be there. I'll text Nick now. Is Aunt T going?" Brooke realized this was probably a silly question. Aunt T and Carol were practically inseparable, having become as close to best friends as two women in different decades could become.

"We are on our way now to pick her up for breakfast. I am just going to kidnap her for the day." Carol again chuckled, her laughter filling Brooke's speakers like music.

"I'm not responsible for how much wine is consumed before you get here!" Benji yelled into the phone. Brooke heard what she could only assume was Carol's hand hitting his arm. "Ouch! So, how's work?"

"No shop talk!" Brooke again heard Carol's hand make contact with Benji's arm.

"Actually, Benji, are you free today to stop by? I would love to talk through this latest case with you. I feel like I am missing something." Brooke couldn't believe she hadn't thought of this before.

"Sure, I'll drop the girls off at home after breakfast and head in."

"Perfect—thank you! And I'll see you guys tonight."

* * *

Brooke walked into the station and was greeted by June

and Dan standing at the front desk. Dan had his phone out, no doubt showing pictures of his three beautiful girls.

"Kat's feeling better now that she is farther along. Once Ellie is feeling better, I am sure she will be by." Dan turned to Brooke. "Hey, boss."

Brooke smirked. Even though they were partners now, Dan still occasionally called her boss. She wasn't sure at this point if it was a nickname or a sign of respect. "Hey, *partner*." Brooke emphasized the last word. Dan rolled his eyes.

June looked at the two of them. "Would you like to inform Detective Hill who called this morning or should I?" There was no missing June's amusement.

"Oh, I would never want to miss an opportunity to let Brooke know that her good friend Greg Levine just called." Dan and June were displaying way too much joy with sharing this information.

Greg Levine was a high-powered attorney. He specialized in criminal defense but also dabbled in family law from time to time. Greg was uber annoying and full of himself, fitting every negative stereotype of lawyers. Brooke had been forced to deal with him on her last big case, she'd been hoping for more time to pass before having to deal with him again.

Brooke rolled her eyes and sighed as if she'd been holding her breath for days. "You know, partner, you could have taken the call because whatever case he is calling about it is our shared case now." Brooke poked Dan as she spoke.

"I would never deny you the privilege of speaking to your friend Greg." Dan couldn't help but to burst out laughing when he said *friend.*

"Thanks so much," Brooke said as she turned to June. "I'm expecting Brian Keenan from the Commonwealth Attorney's Office. Can you send him back to our office when he signs in?"

Brooke turned and started walking down the hallway alongside Dan. She noticed his raised his eyebrow. "Did he meet with the brother already?"

"He did, and said he wanted to talk first thing this morning," Brooke said as she walked into her office.

Dan sat down at his desk, opposite Brooke. "Interesting." He leaned back and smiled. "Want me to stay or go when he comes?"

Brooke threw a pen at him. "Stay."

"Okay, okay. Hey, I was talking to Kat a little bit about the case, and she reminded me that one of our old college friends now works for ICE. I know you have a contact through Brian, but I thought I would reach out to my guy this morning." Dan picked the pen up and placed it on Brooke's desk.

"That would be great, actual—" Brooke was interrupted by a knock on the open door.

"Sorry, I know I'm early. Is now a good time?" Brian

stood in the doorway, looking very handsome in another navy suit.

"Yes, absolutely. Just give me a minute." Brooke moved a couple of boxes from the corner of the room so Brian would have space to stand inside. She motioned for Brian to the corner. "Brian, I'm not sure if you remember Dan Beal. He is my partner here in all this chaos." The two men nodded to one another.

"Hi, Brian. We've met," Dan confirmed.

Her mind skidded into another direction as the two men briefly caught up, and Brooke remembered she still had yet to type a text out to Nick about dinner. She typed out a quick text to him: *Dinner at the Nobles tonight?*

Brooke leaned back at her desk and turned her attention to both men. "Okay, sorry. I am all yours."

Brian and Dan wore matching raised eyebrow expressions.

CHAPTER 15

Brian left the corner he had been standing in and perched himself on the edge of Brooke's desk. *We've got to figure out a better arrangement in here.* Brooke shook her head at the thought. The office was not working out, already crammed with two desks and an ancient filing cabinet. There was nowhere for someone else to be while meeting with her and Dan.

"I texted Drew after I spoke to you at the courthouse." Brian cleared his throat. "He texted back right away and said he was free—last night. We met at the King's Street Tavern."

Good place, Brooke mused. The tavern was located near the Hilton in Alexandria and wouldn't be crowded, a place where it would be easy to hear a conversation, unlike some of Alexandria's more crowded bars.

Brooke looked around for something to write with and noticed Dan was already taking notes. *Thank God for Dan.* Brooke was grateful he was one step ahead of her this morning.

"Honestly, it was mainly just catching up until he asked me if I had heard about his brother." Brian paused for dramatic effect. "I didn't lie to him. I told him that I met with his wife and the detective who was helping her secure a protective order."

"How did he take it?" Dan raised his eyebrows as he looked up from his notes.

"Better than I would have thought. It didn't seem to faze him at all. He just kept saying, 'Yeah, Matt's changed a lot. Then he started talking about Catalina. . .. We spent more time talking about her than his brother." Brian frowned while saying the last part.

"Judging by your face, I'm guessing you found this odd?" Brooke tilted her head.

"Very. Look, I get high school was a long time ago, but Drew and Matt were so close. It's hard to believe Matt has changed that much. Drew had a lot of sympathy for Catalina and didn't seem happy with his parents for siding with Matt." Brian looked from Brooke to Dan.

"I'm not a parent, but don't they normally side with their kids?" Brooke asked.

"Yes," Dan answered immediately.

"Did he say if there was a rift in the family? Witness any abuse?" Dan continued to jot notes as he spoke.

"Not exactly. Judging by the way he spoke about Matt and his parents; I would say there was. He never outright said he saw anything." Brian looked at his watch. "I'm getting bombarded with texts right now from the office. I'm going to have to go. Are you coming tomorrow?"

Dan and Brooke looked at each other.

"The protective order hearing. It's set for tomorrow. The judge wouldn't give her the two weeks." Brian was starting to get up.

"That's not normal." Dan looked at Brooke for confirmation.

"No, it's not. I can only think of one other time this happened in my career." Brooke turned from Dan to Brian. Brooke was studying Brian's reaction to this unprecedented procedure. Staring just a second too long, Brian turned his face to face her and smirked.

"So, she didn't mention this to you?" Brian asked Brooke.

"No, but to be fair, I didn't ask. I assumed the order was for two weeks not forty-eight hours. We will be there. Are you the attorney?" Brooke's phone buzzed on her desk. It was Nick. Brooke noticed Brian glancing at her phone.

"No. They just need a Commonwealth representative in the courtroom. It's not me, it's my colleague, Emma Wright. I'll be there, though, just not in the courtroom." Brian looked at his watch. "I've got to run. I'll see you both tomorrow."

"Thanks, Brian!" Brooke said as he walked out.

Dan and Brooke looked at each other. "So, tomorrow?" Dan asked.

"I know," Brooke answered. "Actually, I don't know. I feel like if I read the report on this case, with Brian's information, too, it makes sense . . ."

"But then you go over the interactions with the victim, and you question everything," Dan finished her thought for her.

"Exactly." Brooke hit her desk. Her strike jolted her phone, and it lit up. She quickly checked the message from Nick. *Sounds great. I should be able to make it there around 7. Love you.*

"I think I better call my contact at ICE," Dan broke Brooke's distracted squirrel-moment with the sound of his voice.

She put her phone in her pocket and shook her head to bring herself back from thinking about Nick. "Yeah, that would be great. It's probably better for you to call someone you already have a relationship with. I am very curious to hear if he can find out anything."

"Sorry, I'm still on this protective order. I know I should have asked her, that's on me. But I am wondering why the judge granted a protective order for forty-eight hours instead of two weeks." Dan rubbed his chin as he spoke. "I honestly have never heard of a judge doing that to a victim who shows up in person. It is normally a here-you-go or a firm no. I didn't even know they could do that. I thought the emergency orders we provided were the only ones for 48 hours."

"You're right. Normally they give them for two weeks or nothing at all. I wonder what she said to the judge to get a protective order for such a short amount of time?" Brooke was leaning on her desk talking to him.

"The judge probably felt the same way we do about this case. Everything checks out until you talk to the victim." Dan was now mimicking Brooke and leaning towards her.

"Do you think it's a cultural thing?" Brooke asked. "The way she acts?"

"Honestly, no. One of Kat's best friends is from Colombia. Yeah, she has a temper sometimes, but she doesn't turn her emotions on and off the way Catalina does." Dan had picked up his phone. "I'm going to text Marcus—that's my friend who works at ICE—then run home and check on Kat, and then call him on my way back if he is available."

"I heard you tell June that Ellie is sick. Sorry . . . I meant to ask if she was okay." Brooke made a mental note to try to be better about asking Dan about his family and connecting on a personal level.

"No worries, and she is fine. Has some bug, but I feel bad for Kat. She isn't sleeping, both from pregnancy and now having a sick toddler. I'm going to go pick her up a coffee. You need anything?" Dan asked as he stood up.

Brooke smiled. *Dan is really such a nice guy.* "I'm good, thanks. Give Kat my love—but from a distance. I don't want any of those germs in here." Brooke motioned around at their office.

As Dan walked out, Brooke picked up her phone to typed out a reply to Nick when June paged her on the office phone. There was no ignoring her British chuckle as she said, "Sorry to disturb you, Detective, but Greg Levine is on hold for you."

97

CHAPTER 16

Brooke took a deep breath. Her first encounter with Greg Levine still haunted her. She'd been a young rookie patrol officer, appearing in court for the first time. Even though their most recent interaction went much smoother, Brooke hated that this slimy lawyer still made her nervous.

"Hi, Greg," Brooke picked up the phone. She heard him let out a laugh.

"If you call me 'Greg,' does that mean I can address you as Brooke? You may recall the last time we spoke; you corrected me by calling yourself Detective Hill." His smugness oozed out of the phone.

Brooke chose to ignore his comment. "What can I do for you?" She had a sinking suspicion about why he was calling her; she was afraid she was right, and he would soon tell her that he was representing Matt Hall.

"I'm calling about a case I heard you were involved in . . ." Greg started by saying.

Don't say Matt Hall. Don't say Matt Hall. Brooke offered up a silent prayer. "Lord, please no."

"Matt and Catalina Hall. I understand she came in

yesterday, and you escorted her down to the courthouse to get a protective order. I don't think I ever heard of your predecessor escorting alleged victims down to the courthouse. Is this a new policy I should be aware of?"

Brooke could tell from the tone of his voice that he thought he had her cornered.

"*Greg*, as I have told you before, I am not going to comment on any ongoing cases." Brooke hoped she'd conveyed her sentiments in a calm, controlled tone. She was working hard at it.

"Says she was only granted a protective order for forty-eight hours. Doesn't that strike you as odd? I think I have only experienced this once before," Greg continued with his *I gotcha* tone.

"Again, Greg, I am not going to comment." Brooke was getting annoyed. It was the reason she kept using his first name. He knew she wouldn't comment on any of this. So, what was the point? To let her know he knew all this information? She wanted to ask, but did not want to engage this man in a back and forth.

"Doesn't matter, I guess. The protective order is going to get thrown out," he said smugly.

"Why do you say that?" Brooke hated to admit it, but she was worried about that too.

"Are you honestly telling me you're not thinking that? Besides, the wife is a nut job," the attorney said with a self-satisfied laugh.

"You're entitled to your opinion. I guess we will find

out tomorrow. I have to say, though, I am surprised Mr. Hall has retained you as his attorney." Brooke couldn't help herself. She didn't want to engage him, but on the other hand, she wanted to make sure he knew he did not have the upper hand. And that she wasn't intimidated by him.

"He hasn't retained me. I told him I would give him advice on how to handle this and see what I can find out." Greg was very matter of fact, suddenly professional.

"Sounds like he is another one of your close personal friends." Brooke chose her words carefully. They were the exact words Greg had said to her months before, on her first case after making detective. It is how he had described his relationship with her predecessor and friend Benji. Benji, however, had not shared the sentiment.

"Hardly. Just doing a favor for one of my other partners. I think he plays golf or something with Matt's dad, Bill. Anyway, I've got to run, I've probably said too much anyway. I'll be in touch after court tomorrow if need be."

"You aren't going to the hearing?" Brooke was surprised.

"No point. It is going to get thrown out—"

"What, now you're friends with the judge too?" Brooke slapped her hand over her mouth. She'd lost control. Thankfully, Greg was still talking and didn't seem to hear her.

"Once it does, I will see how they want to proceed." With that, Greg Levine hung up.

"Ugh! That man!" Brooke exclaimed to no one but herself. She hated that he could get under her skin like that.

Brooke took another deep breath. *I have to focus on*

something else to get the taste of that jerk out of my mouth! She settled on doing some electronic cleanup of a few of her cases, which still needed to be done. After turning on her computer, she began the mundane task. And before she knew it, Dan walked back in.

Brooke looked up from her computer. "How's Ellie feeling? How's Kat holding up?"

Dan sat down in his chair. "Both are emotional." He let out a little sigh as he said this.

"Sorry." Brooke realized when it came to parenting, she had little to contribute to the conversation. "Did you get a hold of your friend Mike, the one who works at ICE?"

"Marcus," Dan corrected her. "I did."

"And?" Brooke gestured with her hand for him to continue.

Dan smiled. "Just wanted to keep you guessing for a minute." Brooke frowned. "I talked to him. He didn't know her by name, nor was he involved in her case, but he looked into her case file for me." Dan took a sip of water before continuing. "They picked her up last week after several anonymous tip calls. And by several, I mean they got three to four calls about her *daily* for two weeks."

"Wow. Really?" Brooke was both surprised and confused. This was an odd thing. "Did they say what the callers complained about?"

"Various things and the information in the file did not list every claim, but there were quite a few things listed—everything from prostitution to selling drugs." Dan raised his eyebrows at her when he finished his sentence.

Brooke tapped her pen on her desk while she was thinking. "Did Marcus happen to say if the reports specified if the callers were male or female?" Brooke tilted her head.

"He didn't. Why? What are you thinking?" Dan asked, mimicking Brooke with a head tilt of his own.

Brooke continued to tap her pen. "I don't know. I can't quite connect all the moving pieces to this case—just wondering if the reports stated it."

"Brooke, I love you, but if you don't stop tapping that pen, I will take it and throw it at you." Dan smiled while he spoke to her.

"Sorry, nervous habit." Brooke shook her head. "Thanks for calling him. Any chance he can send us the files?"

"Already asked. He's sending them, but he warned me they will probably be heavily redacted."

"Figures." Brooke rolled her eyes.

There was a knock on their open door, and Officer D'Augusto, one of the station's patrol officers, stood in the doorway. Brooke didn't know him well, just that he was often paired with Nick. Brooke liked to joke with Nick about how they must call them the "pretty boy team" when they were together. Gavin D'Augusto was ruggedly handsome. Tall, dark hair and beard, with almost caramel-colored eyes. The eyes are what stood out.

"Hey, guys, sorry to interrupt," he said as he walked

a foot into their office. It's all the space he had. "I just responded to a DV call and wanted to brief one of you."

"I got it," Dan volunteered. "I'll meet you in the front conference room since there is nowhere to sit in this cell." Dan gestured to the cramped space.

As Dan and Officer D'Augusto walked out, Dan turned to Brooke. "By the way, boss, you look exhausted. Are you sleeping, okay?"

Brooke looked up, not really knowing how to answer his question, especially on the fly like that. No, she wasn't sleeping. She couldn't even remember if she'd had any coffee yet. "Telling someone they look tired is another way to tell them they look awful, Dan."

Officer D'Augusto, who'd only made it a couple yards down the hallway, laughed, and Dan put his hands up in surrender. "I would never. Just concerned about your sleep schedule."

The two men strode toward the conference room. For the first time that day, Brooke paused—and realized how tired she truly was.

CHAPTER 17

Brooke woke up, startled and wondering where she was before seeing Benji standing in front of her, laughing. "Don't worry, it's happened to me before."

Brooke tried to regain her full bearings. She had put her head down on her desk for just a minute, or at least, she thought it was a minute. Brooke looked up at the clock. It had been a half-hour since Dan had left their office.

"Sorry." Brooke felt groggy. She slapped her left cheek then her right side to try to wake herself up. *Guess I really am sleep deprived.*

"Do you want to just talk tonight?" Benji looked around for a place to sit. He settled on taking over Dan's desk.

"I know. It's extra cramped in here now." Brooke had read Benji's mind. Though, it hadn't been hard. "Now's good. Sorry, I guess I'm more tired than I realized."

Benji looked concerned. Brooke put her hand up. "Do *not* summon the troops. I am fine—I am just tired." Benji continued to stare at her. "I really am!"

"Okay, okay. I would have been here sooner, but I was a little concerned about leaving those two alone." Brooke knew Benji was referring to Carol and Aunt T.

"How many bottles down are they?" she asked. Her aunt and Carol were known for their wine habit, which grew exponentially when they were together.

Benji put two fingers up. "I left them on the couch. They had just turned on the Hallmark Channel."

Brooke laughed. After all that Aunt T had given up for Brooke and Cassie, Brooke was happy she had found a kindred spirit in Carol.

"Okay, lay it on me. What are you so preoccupied with?" Benji was never one for beating around the bush.

"It's this weird case we have right now. We were called there the other night for potential stalking, no evidence. Victim showed up yesterday morning—an immigrant. I don't know, everything else is just not adding up, either." Brooke grabbed one of the many half drank plastic water bottles on her desk and to take a sip.

Benji's eyes encouraged her to keep talking. She obliged. "The presumed victim came in yesterday morning. Not a citizen but married to a citizen and just had a baby. She came in with her aunt, implied her husband called ICE on her and had just recently been detained in Farmville because of it. Told Dan and me her husband was the one who got her out and now is keeping her from their son. She claimed her husband is cheating on her and that she has been abused, but gave no specifics on either. She brought pictures showing how he is stalking her now too. Seemed to have legitimate fear about it all." Brooke put her elbow on her desk and rested her chin in her hand.

"Protective order?" Benji asked.

"I took her to the courthouse to get the protective order. She met with a representative from the Juvenile and Domestic Relations office. I also had Brian Keenan from the Commonwealth's office there to walk her through it and ensure she got appropriate resources."

There was a pause. "Wanted the Commonwealth's opinion or just an excuse to see Brian?" Benji raised his eyebrows at her.

Brooke threw her pen at him. "Opinion. He had the same feelings I did. Something is off. She got a protective order but only for forty-eight hours—odd, right? We go back to court tomorrow." She paused but didn't close her mouth.

Benji looked at her, "There's more?"

"There is. There are a lot of moving pieces with this case. Brian met with the husband's brother, an old friend, who didn't have the nicest things to say about the husband, his brother. Also, odd. Family normally being thicker and all. Dan Beal," Brooke nodded at the computer in front of Benji, referring to her partner, "called his ICE contact and was told they received three to four tip calls a day for two weeks on the victim. . .. I don't know what I am missing, but there's something." Brooke crossed her arms.

"I don't know that much about ICE detainment. Does the person who is detained know how the agents found them?" Benji leaned back in Dan's chair as he spoke.

"Meaning, is there any way the victim would have known how the agents were tipped off? Anonymous calls but by one specific person?"

"You think she knows they were anonymous calls but is blaming her husband or knows her husband is the anonymous caller?" Brooke asked.

"I'm not sure. I'm just wondering out loud." Benji looked up. "Any ideas on why the judge only granted a protective order for forty-eight hours?"

"No." Brooke took a deep breath. "And the victim didn't tell me how long the protective order was good for. I assumed it was for the normal two-week span. Oh, and here is the best part: Greg Levine is giving the husband free legal advice."

"Ha!" Benji laughed. "I do not miss dealing with that clown. Have you thought about following her and/or the husband?"

"I don't know that there is enough to warrant that, do you? I can't imagine getting clearance for that level of investigation yet." Brooke looked up at the ceiling, matching Benji's brainstorming posture, as she thought about this option more.

Dan reappeared in their office just then with Officer D'Augusto behind him. "Benji, it's good to see you. You remember Gavin D'Augusto?" Benji stood up, and the three men shook hands.

"I was just asking Benji his thoughts on the case. He

brought up possibly following Catalina and Matt." Brooke said to catch Dan up.

"I don't think we would get the clearance, at least not yet. What do you think, Benji?" Dan turned his attention to Benji.

"It will be interesting to see what happens in court tomorrow. Other than that, I think you probably have all the information you are going to get right now. If I learned anything over the years, it was that when something doesn't seem right with a case, it normally isn't. And if there are holes, the holes will grow as you investigate further." Benji looked at his watch. "Sorry, I couldn't be more helpful. I know it's easier to say, but I wouldn't worry too much about this. You both will figure it out." Benji started to get up. "I have to head back, make sure the house is still standing. Brooke, I'll see you tonight. Beal, D 'Augusto, good to see you both." Benji hit the backs of both men like a coach might after a great play before walking out.

"I guess we wait to see what happens tomorrow and then come up with a plan," Brooke said, looking at Dan. He nodded in agreement.

"I have to head out too. Brooke, tell Simons we missed him today." Officer D'Augusto turned away.

"What do you mean?" Brooke was confused. *Come to think of it, he said he was going to stop by.*

"He called out sick at like 4:00 a.m. Must be bad. I

haven't known the guy to take a sick day *ever.* Hope you don't catch whatever it is." Officer D'Augusto turned again and walked down the hallway.

Me either, thought Brooke. Out of the corner of her eye, she caught Dan scrutinizing her.

CHAPTER 18

Benji and Carol Noble's house looked like it had been picked up from an old New England town and plopped down in Alexandria, Virginia. With a nod to Colonial America, the décor inside, including a fireplace in every room, made it the most inviting house Brooke had ever been in. It was a home that brought her peace and joy when she thought of all the shared dinners and holidays, she had experienced over the past few years here. She took a deep breath to settle her nerves. She did not want the three people on the other side of the door to have any indication something was bothering her—because something was. And she wasn't ready to talk about it yet. Her thoughts immediately turned to Nick, and the irony of her not being ready to talk hit her like a heavyweight punch.

Brooke had texted Nick on her way to Benji and Carol's house. He'd texted immediately back and said he was stuck on a call but should be there soon. She knew he was lying; she knew he had not gone to work today. *It is a small station. Doesn't he worry that someone will say something to me?*

Brooke arrived at "Chalet de Peace" and turned off her car in the Nobles' driveway. Then she tapped the Facetime icon, selected the first person, then added a second line. Then she waited for everyone to answer so the three-way video call could start. In seconds, Jacs's and Cassie's faces appeared.

"Clearly, he is so busy worrying about covering up whatever he is hiding that he isn't thinking."

While Cassie and Jacs took turns bashing Nick for hiding something, then reassuring Brooke everything was going to be okay, Brooke became lost in her own thoughts. Jac's words from the other night replayed in her head.

Cassie, apparently sensing her sister's hiatus, brought Brooke back. "Look, sis, he's hiding something, and I am so sorry that he is acting like this." Cassie was in her dressing room, half made up for that night's show. "Whatever it is, you will be okay. I know you know that."

Brooke hung up as she approached the Nobles' front porch. She took another calming breath in and rang the doorbell.

The door opened within seconds. "Why on earth are you ringing the doorbell? You know to just walk in or use the key we gave you." Carol's warmth enveloped Brooke as soon as Brooke saw her. "Did you lose the spare key again? Or was that, Cassie? I can't remember now," she said with a little Southern-twinged giggle.

"Definitely Cassie." Brooke hugged Carol as she walked in. Brooke sniffed the air, where the distinct smell of

Chinese food had filled the house. "I thought we were doing pizza tonight." Brooke heard the sound of Benji and her aunt laughing.

"There was a change of plans." Carol winked at her as she led her into the massive kitchen.

"Tell her the truth, Carol." Benji chuckled as he admonished his wife. Seated at the farm style table was Benji and Aunt T. Brooke smiled and rushed to hug her aunt. She did not realize until that moment how much she needed the comfort of seeing her mother-figure. Aunt T was in her signature black yoga pants, an oversized sweater, and her toffee-colored hair was piled up in a top knot. She was effortlessly beautiful, as always.

Carol threw the kitchen towel that had been resting on her shoulder at Benji. "Talia and I took a little siesta this afternoon, and we simply did not feel like cooking," Carol said as she grabbed the towel back and snapped it at Benji with a flick of her wrist.

"So, she bought out the whole Chinese restaurant instead!" Benji took a sip of his whiskey and was jolted when Carol punched him in the arm.

"Where's Nick?" Aunt T asked, looking around. Almost right on cue, the doorbell rang.

"Apparently, here." Brooke turned toward the front door.

As she walked to the door, Benji yelled, "Unless it's more Chinese. I think Carol may have forgotten to order one or two things." Benji was cracking himself up at this.

Brooke opened the door, and there stood Nick. Even though he had put her through so much stress over the past few days, she still felt so much love for this man. Dressed in his trademark white T-shirt and a pair of dark jeans, he kissed her cheek. "Hi, beautiful. I missed you."

She kissed him back. But he broke away and looked at her. "Chinese?"

Brooke laughed. "Don't ask—also Carol and Aunt T have been drinking all day." She figured the warning was warranted.

They walked toward the kitchen hand in hand. "Thanks for the heads-up," Nick said, squeezing her hand.

"Nick!" Carol and Talia said in unison.

Benji stood up to shake his hand. "Good, now that Simons is here, let's eat."

Benji wasn't kidding, once the food was set out on the long farm-style table, it looked like Carol had indeed bought out the local Chinese takeout place. "I don't know. . . do we have enough food for all of us?" Aunt T smiled as she handed a glass of wine to Brooke.

Brooke did her best to forget Nick's recent behavior and relax. Doing so made it an enjoyable night, filled with laughter. And she needed that. Nick was more himself than he had been recently.

"You work today?" Benji asked Nick pointedly. Brooke looked at Nick to assess his reaction. She wondered if Benji knew something or was he just asking to ask. Sometimes,

Benji heard things, simply by staying engaged with his old "family" at the station.

Nick launched into a detailed description about his day. Brooke had to look down. *Did he rehearse this?* Brooke thought. *Maybe he is waiting till they were alone to tell me the truth.* A part of her knew this was wishful thinking. He's already lied to her on the text message.

Brooke picked her head up when Nick said he was with D'Augusto for most of the day. At that moment, she couldn't help herself. "Did you respond to the DV call he had?"

Nick glanced at her. She could see it all start to register on his face, that he had been caught in his web of lies. "No, I was responding to an accident off Beulah."

"DV call? Anything more than just a call?" Aunt T asked Brooke. Brooke held her gaze with Nick for another second, then turned toward Aunt T. She wanted him to know she knew he was lying. She wanted him to fret over.

"As of right now, I don't think so. Dan was the one briefed on it." Brooke took a bite of her egg roll.

"How do you like having a partner, sweetheart?" Carol put more rice on Brooke's plate without asking. Carol's love language was feeding the ones she cared about.

As Brooke was about to tell the group how great it was to have Dan, Nick's phone rang. He looked down, and instantly, a panicked look flashed on his face. A mixture of dread and stress. "Sorry, I have to take this." He stood up and walked toward the front door.

As the front door closed, Benji, Carol, and Aunt T stared at Brooke. "Brooke," Aunt T's voice had taken on a low, serious tone. "Is everything okay?"

Benji answered before Brooke could, "She's fine, Talia. Just distracted with one of her cases—she has to go to court tomorrow. Right, Brooke?" Benji narrowed his eyes, willing her to go along with him. She figured he knew it was more than that, but in this moment, she was grateful for his rescue.

"Yeah, actually when Nick gets back, I hope you aren't offended if we leave. I'm exhausted and have to be in court first thing tomorrow morning." Brooke gave a nod toward Benji as a way to thank him without the others noticing.

"Of course—you need rest. Do you want to take any leftovers?" Carol asked as they heard the front door open and shut again. Nick appeared before them. He opened his mouth to say something, but again, Benji interrupted.

"Simons, Brooke was just saying she's exhausted and was going to head home. Can you drive her? I'll bring Talia back to her place in Brooke's car and then drop it off at her house." Brooke wasn't sure how Benji knew that something was going on and that Nick and Brooke needed to talk. But it was obvious he did. She was grateful for this second unnecessary gesture.

"I'm fine, really, Benji," Brooke tried to protest. "Plus, how are you going to get home from my house?"

"Regardless of what you and your sister think, I have

become skilled with small electronic devices and can easily call an Uber," Benji said with a smile.

"Thank you for everything. Do you need help clearing?" Nick asked Carol as Brooke stood up.

"No, just get our girl home safely." Aunt T raised her glass.

"I will." Nick put his hand over his heart as a pledge. "I promise."

Brooke and Nick headed out the front door and made their way to his truck parked in the driveway. Brooke said a silent prayer that this second car conversation would go better than the first.

CHAPTER 19

Nick had not stop to open her door as he normally does. Instead, he continued around the front of the car to the driver's side door, unlocked the car, and got in.

Silence ensued as Nick and Brooke made their way through Benji and Carol's neighborhood. The tension in the truck was palpable. Brooke tried hard not to break first. But the deafening silence after seven minutes was too much for her, she spoke first.

"Are we going to talk about this or continue in silence for the last five minutes to my house?" Brooke hoped she hadn't come off as snarky as it sounded to her ears.

"Talk about what?" Nick seemed genuinely confused, making Brooke lose all patience.

"You can't be serious?" Brooke tried to stifle her swirling emotions, realizing they wouldn't help but likely would cause Nick to get defensive. This car ride's emotion was anger rather than sadness, and she knew it was seeping through every word she spoke. She tried to regroup in her mind.

"Okay, well clearly you have something to say." Nick glanced at her while driving, and judging by his tone,

Brooke realized she was not the only one in the truck trying to keep anger in check.

"Are we going to talk about the phone calls?" Brooke tried to sound sincere, not annoyed.

"That you clearly told everyone about?" Nick's tone was filled with rage now.

"No, I didn't. I don't know why Benji insisted that you drive me home." Brooke hated that she sounded like she was pleading with him to believe her.

"Right." Nick continued to stare straight ahead and drive.

Brooke was done putting up with his demeaning attitude. "Maybe it was because everyone could see the dread come across your face as you looked at your ringing phone." She turned her body to face him.

"I told you already; I am not ready to talk about it," he said in an icy tone.

"That's not going to cut it anymore, Nick. This is affecting us, our relationship." Brooke was pleading now.

Nick ran his fingers through his hair. "You have no idea," he mumbled.

"What?" Brooke wasn't sure she heard him correctly.

"Nothing," Nick said. He was trying to tamp down the conflict by putting his hand on her leg. "Can we just drop it, please? I'm not ready."

Brooke moved his hand from her leg. "No, Nick. We need to talk about whatever is going on now."

Nick didn't say anything. He simply looked straight ahead, as they turned onto Brooke's road.

"Did you hear me?" Brooke asked as he turned into her driveway.

Nick parked the car. "I don't get it. We talked this morning, and you were all 'I trust you. You can tell me when you're ready.'" Nick spoke in a mocking tone, trying to emulate a child's voice. It was downright cruel.

"You don't need to be mean." Brooke turned her head to face out the passenger window. She was determined not to release any tears again tonight.

"It's the truth." It was Nick's turn to face her. "What changed?"

Brooke swung around, almost violently, to face him. "You cannot honestly be asking me that!"

Nick looked confused.

He can't be serious right now. She could feel the effects of the adrenaline racing through her blood vessels as her anger mounted. Her cheeks felt warm, and there was a distant pounding in her ears. "How was *work*, Nick?" She knew how nasty she sounded, asking him this, and hated to admit that she also no longer cared how she came across.

"We already talked about it at the Nobles. Why are you asking me again?" Nick turned to look forward again.

Brooke was dumbfounded. "Okay. Fine. Gavin D'Augusto stopped by to brief Dan about the DV call he ran. When he was leaving, he asked me to tell you to feel better. He said it must be bad because he can't remember another time when you called out sick." Brooke paused. "I can't either and was pretty surprised to hear it."

Nick said nothing. Brooke waited. She was determined to wait him out this time.

"I didn't realize you were my mother now. Next time, I'll let you know so you can write me a note." He turned toward her as he spoke. His eyes were slits, his rage swelling.

Brooke felt the tears well up as the force of his sarcasm hit her.

She willed herself to ignore this comment. "The calls, the way you are acting, the lies, the not showing up for work . . . I don't know who you are anymore."

"I didn't just *not* show up. I told you this morning that I barely slept. I needed to sleep, to think—I needed a day. I didn't realize in addition to letting the station know, I also needed to clear it through you." There was no coming back, no walking the mean-spirited words back.

So, Brooke pressed forward. "You don't, but it's weird. All of this is weird—can you not see that?" Brooke couldn't understand why he didn't see her point.

"And once again we are arguing in your driveway about this." Nick was shaking his head.

"You think this is how I want to end my night? I don't understand why you can't see how concerning all of this is to me. How it is affecting us."

Nick didn't move.

"Nick, look at me!" she finally shouted.

Nick ignored her and continued to face forward, apparently waiting for her to get out of his truck.

"Nick!" Brooke reached out for his forearm, but he pulled away.

"I can't do this. I don't want to go over this again. You need to give me space." The volume of his voice had lowered to a near-whisper, but his tone had not changed.

"Nick, look at me." Brooke was crying.

"I can't right now." Nick lowered his head to his lap. "I need to go home. I need you to give me space. I'll call you when I am ready to talk about this."

"What?" Brooke was sobbing now. "Why are you acting like I did something wrong?"

"I just need to clear my head, and I need space." Nick took a deep breath in. "I need you to give me that."

"What about what I need, Nick? This isn't just a one-way relationship!" Brooke started yelling through her crying.

"I understand, but right now I need to think about what I need." His voice cracked. "I think I should go."

Brooke was in disbelief. She felt a mixture of deep sadness and what she thought was righteous anger. She reached for the door handle but then turned. "Nick?" She didn't know what she was going to say after his name . . . she just wanted reassurance of some kind.

He finally looked at her. It was his turn for his eyes to fill with tears. "I'll call you in a few days."

Brooke opened the door. She couldn't stay in the truck any longer. Her lungs wouldn't expand.

As soon as she walked a few feet away from the truck, Nick put it in reverse and was gone before she could catch her breath.

CHAPTER 20

Brooke had another restless night's sleep. She kept replaying her conversation with Nick in her head, and when her mind was not on that, it was on the sinking feeling that she was missing something big with Catalina Hall's domestic violence case.

* * *

Cassie's screams are earsplitting.

All I see is orange, all I hear is the distinct popping of flames.

Where's Mommy? She was right here. My thoughts spiral.

Cassie screams some more.

Mommy's going to come any minute. She has to.

Where is she . . .

* * *

Brooke bolted upright in bed, her heart racing inside her chest, with both legs feeling numb. The nightmare from her childhood had enveloped her once again. She glanced at the clock: 6:05 a.m. *Crap!* Her alarm had never gone off. *Did I even set it?* she wondered. After her conversation with Nick, she wouldn't be shocked to learn she had forgotten.

Racing around her house, trying to get ready, never worked out well for her. Brooke kept tripping over household objects and just couldn't seem to find anything this morning. She had meant to get up an hour before—this was not how she wanted to start her day.

She checked her phone and saw she had one message and one missed call. Brooke couldn't help it—she'd been hoping to hear from Nick. So, when she saw both communications were from Dan, her heart sank a bit.

Crazy morning here—okay if we meet at the courthouse? Dan had typed out.

Okay, good. That gave her the little extra time she needed. Taking a deep breath in, she walked toward her kitchen and debated if she wanted coffee or tea. She decided on tea because tea felt more comforting to her and that was what she needed. Comfort. She smirked to herself and shook her head. Comfort from which part of her disastrous last forty-eight hours. The Nick part? The awful dream that crept into her life when she was stressed part? The case part?

She reached in the cabinet and grabbed a teabag from Aunt T's favorite box. She could picture her aunt in her sun-filled kitchen, with her hair in a top knot and her red glasses at the tip of her nose, sipping her cuppa and talking to her cat, Cookie, and her plants. Brooke smiled at the visualization.

Brooke took her mug into her bedroom. Once she sipped her tea, she instantly felt calmer. She had an extra fifteen minutes she hadn't been counting on, and that calmed her down as well. As her heart rate slowed, she picked up all the items she had tripped over, straightened up her room, and got dressed.

This was the easy morning I was hoping for, she thought to herself as she put on the finishing touches to her natural-inspired makeup. She walked into the kitchen and put her teacup in the sink. Brooke checked her phone again. Still nothing from Nick. She didn't know what to expect, but she knew the likelihood of him contacting her this soon was slim. A part of her had hoped to wake up to an "I'm so sorry for the way I acted" text again. The realization that this was where their relationship stood made her want to cry again.

Looking out her kitchen window, she saw a red cardinal land on her patio furniture. Aunt T had always said that if a red cardinal crossed your path, it is meant to give you strength and hope. Brooke didn't know if Aunt T was making it up or not, but at this moment, she chose to believe it. Believe that this was her sign that everything was going to be okay—everything in her life.

Brooke looked at her smartwatch and realized she should have left two minutes ago. She grabbed a protein bar and took one last look in the mirror. Court appearances always meant a little more dress-up than everyday attire. Brooke wore her "court dress," as she called it. Her simple J Crew gray-sheath dress with her mother's blue-gray pearl necklace. With the added time, she had straightened her shoulder length brown hair. As she slipped on her black heels, it dawned on her that there was a good chance her car was still at the Nobles'.

Brooke grabbed her things and peered through the door leading to the carport and saw her car. As she approached it, she saw a yellow note on the dash. Brooke grabbed the note. Benji's unmistakable chicken-scratch handwriting covered the yellow, lined paper.

I told you I would have your car back to you. I also put gas in it. And your maintenance required light is on.

Brooke smiled. *Always taking on the role of my protector.* She grabbed the note and threw it in her bag. She was about to get in her car when Dan Beal beeped his horn at her. He was in his black Jeep Grand Cherokee, pulling into her driveway.

Brooke turned. "What's that line from *Mean Girls?*" he yelled at her.

Brooke laughed. "'Get in loser, we're going shopping.'"

"Get in loser, we're going to court," Dan said with a laugh.

* * *

It had just started to rain as Dan navigated his way through the small town of Fairfax, trying to get to the courthouse. Brooke was relieved that he'd stopped by to pick her up. Riding with Dan was a good distraction from the noise in her head.

"Thank you again for picking me up, Dan. I hate driving in the rain," Brooke said as the drops increased their size and frequency on the windshield, prompting Dan to turn his wipers on full blast.

"You're on the way. I figured I would see if you'd left yet."

Brooke had a sinking suspicion that wasn't the only reason. She decided to poke around. "Have you talked to Nick?" Dan and Nick were somewhat close. They'd all gone through the Police Academy together and then were placed at the same station.

Dan glanced at her. He was dressed in a navy suit that Brooke had no doubt Kat had a hand in picking out. "I don't want to pry, but is everything okay? He hasn't returned any of my texts or calls since this past weekend. And your face when D'Augusto said he called out sick . . . well, you need to work on your poker face, boss."

Brooke nodded. "Funny. And I don't know if everything is okay. He isn't really talking to me, either."

Dan pulled into the government parking garage. "Strange," he said as he parked the Jeep in an open spot.

Within seconds, Catalina and Maria crossed ahead of them to the stairwell.

"Let's wait a minute. I don't want to walk in with them." Brooke turned toward Dan as she spoke, ready to grab his arm should he have not heard her. She had a sinking suspicion that this court hearing was not going to go well, and she wanted to put off dealing with Aunt Maria as long as possible.

CHAPTER 21

B rooke and Dan walked up the two flights of stairs to the lobby for the courtrooms used for juvenile and domestic relations. The lobby was full. They searched for Catalina and her aunt. Brooke spotted Brian Keenan standing by one of the conference rooms, talking to who she assumed was his colleague, Emma Wright.

Brooke knew through the grapevine that Emma was newly out of law school, and Brooke knew Brian was mentoring her. Something about the way he interacted with her made Brooke wonder if there was something else going on between them. The distance between them was narrow, and she was leaning toward him. A pang of jealousy struck Brooke in the heart, followed by the feeling of guilt, knowing she had no right to be jealous. She'd made her choice.

Dan touched Brooke's arm. "Brian's over there," he said as he headed toward Brian and Emma. Brooke followed.

Brian shook hands with both of them. Another pang of hurt coursed through her at how formal this interaction was. She was hoping it was for Emma's sake. "Dan, Brooke, this is my colleague, Emma Wright. I was just briefing her on our meeting with Mrs. Hall."

Emma reached out her petite, manicured hand. Brooke looked into her beautiful brown half-moon-shaped eyes that turned upward as she smiled. "Nice to meet you both." She moved her low-hanging long black ponytail out of her way.

"Will you be in the courtroom?" Dan, speaking to Emma, brought Brooke back from admiring the young attorney's youthful, gorgeous glow. Inside, she berated herself. *Get it together, Hill.*

"Yes. They need a Commonwealth representative. Brian was just making sure I was up to date." Emma turned toward Brian when she said this and smiled. The look in her eyes—it was the unmistakable look of a woman in love, *or at least in lust*, Brooke thought.

"Do either of you know who the judge is?" Brooke asked Brian and Emma.

"Southers," Brian answered.

Brooke wasn't sure if having Vivian Southers presiding over the hearing was a good thing or a bad thing. Judge Southers was well-known for her no-nonsense approach, so Brooke wasn't sure how that would play out with Catalina...or her aunt.

"Have you spoken to Matt Hall?" Dan asked Emma.

"I haven't, and I probably won't. I am just there as a just-in-case person. I believe he is standing right over there, though." Emma pointed over Dan and Brooke's shoulders. Brooke turned to get a peek.

Matt Hall could have been the poster child for the All-American look. His blond hair was styled in a short side part, and he was wearing what looked to be an expertly tailored, expensive gray suit. His muscular physique was evident through the fabric. He'd certainly played sports—perhaps still did. Standing next to him was an older version of Matt, who Brooke assumed was his father. And a woman had her hand on Matt's back. Her cropped, dark hair with streaks of silver was offset by her deep purple dress. *Must be the mother,* Brooke thought. *Wonder if the older brother is.*

As if reading Brooke's thoughts, Brian answered aloud. "Andrew isn't here."

"Interesting." Brooke turned toward Brian. "Have you spoken to him again?"

"No. I haven't talked to Drew since the other night." As Brian answered, Catalina approached them.

"Detective Hill, Detective Beal, thank you for coming." She only addressed Dan and Brooke.

A voice over the speaker announced, "Dorado Hall versus Hall, now in Courtroom A." Catalina's eyes were on Matt and his parents as they walked in. She took a deep breath in, and Brooke put her hand on her shoulder. "Let's go, okay?"

As they entered the courtroom, Dan and Brooke took

seats behind Catalina's aunt. It looked as though she was the only member of Catalina's family in attendance. Next to Catalina sat one of the county's pro bono lawyers. Brooke had seen him before but couldn't remember his name. As Brooke wracked her brain for the name, the courtroom doors opened and in walked Greg Levine. He strolled right up and sat next to Matt Hall.

Shock interrupted her trip into her memory banks. Dan leaned close to Brooke and whispered, "I thought he wasn't coming today."

Brooke shrugged as Judge Southers banged her gavel. "Case number 9806, reviewing a permanent protective order. If I am understanding this correctly, the original was only granted for forty-eight hours by one of my colleagues."

The public defender stood up. "Todd Walters, your honor, and yes, that is correct."

"Mr. Walters, unless your client can convince me otherwise, I am inclined to throw this request out." Judge Southers narrowed her eyes.

"Your honor, my client is fearful. She has been abused, stalked, detained by ICE, and had her son taken away. She—" Todd didn't get to finish his next sentence before Greg was on his feet.

"Objection, your honor, half of what has come out of Mr. Walter's mouth is hearsay. There is no evidence of abuse or stalking. My client did not take her son away. He requested that he and Mrs. Hall seek professional help to work on their relationship. My client had nothing to do with ICE, and if I may approach the bench, I have a copy of the file from ICE that details why they picked up Mrs. Hall—after several anonymous tips." Judge Southers waved Greg to the bench to review the documents.

"Mr. Walter, does your client have any new information that I have not already seen?" Judge Southers seemed to be annoyed. As Todd opened his mouth, she put her hand up. "I've seen the grainy images that your client is claiming are her husband. No one can tell if that is Mr. Hall or Bigfoot."

Catalina looked back at her aunt, who was shifting in her seat. Todd spoke: "No, your honor."

Judge Southers looked from Catalina to Matt. "I want you both to know I do not dismiss protective order cases lightly. However, to issue a permanent protective order, there needs to be concrete evidence. There is none here. Mrs. Hall, this might not seem fair to you, but in terms of the law, you need evidence, not just what you think and feel." Judge Southers banged her gavel. "Case dismissed."

Brooke didn't have time to process what had just happened before the screaming started. As soon as the judge banged her gavel, Catalina and her aunt stood up and shouted together. It was a mix of Spanish and English. It took everyone a minute to comprehend what was happening.

Judge Southers banged her gavel again and yelled, "Order!" The bailiff approached the frantic women, ordering them to calm down. Matt Hall had also stood up and started shouting back at Catalina, telling her it was her fault, not his.

Emma Wright, from the back of the courtroom, dug into her black bag, pulled out a whistle, and blew it. Everyone turned.

"Thank you, Ms. Wright," Judge Southers had a pointed smile looking from the back of the courtroom then to Catalina. "Mrs. Hall, you have exactly one minute to leave my courtroom with this woman"—she pointed to Catalina's aunt— "or I will hold both of you in contempt of court. Just so we are clear, that means going to jail."

Catalina's aunt opened her mouth to say something, but Catalina shot her a death look. Both women got up and walked out.

Judge Southers waited for them to leave and then addressed Greg Levine. "Mr. Levine, you may escort your client out."

As they passed Brooke and Dan, Greg winked at Brooke. It made her stomach turn. She and Dan got up to follow them out. In the lobby, Brooke made a beeline for Emma.

"How in the world did you know to do that and have it not backfire?" Brooke had never seen a whistle used in a courtroom like that. "That was definitely a first."

Emma laughed. "I clerked for Judge Southers one summer. She told me a story about how a courtroom had erupted, and the judge couldn't get everyone back together.

He pulled out a whistle and blew it. She thought it was brilliant. Ever since then, I've carried one."

"Ready to head back to the station?" Dan had walked up behind Brooke.

Brooke looked back at the Halls; they were consoling each other. She then looked at Catalina and her aunt. The look in both of their eyes as they stared down the Halls—*something isn't right . . .*

CHAPTER 22

B rooke checked her phone for what felt like the millionth time on the ride back to the station. Dan turned to her. "He hasn't responded to me, either."

Brooke hated the way she felt. She was mad at Nick. Mad at the way he'd treated her, mad that he was keeping something from her, mad about the lying, and mad that she was feeling like some frantic girl waiting by the phone.

Trying desperately to push Nick out of her mind, she focused on the circus they had just witnessed in court. She just didn't know how to do that. She kept fidgeting, not able to keep from her moving. Her leg tapped along to the movement of the car.

"Can we talk for a minute about what the eff we just witnessed?" Dan said, sensing Brooke needed a change of topic.

Brooke jerked out of her trance. "I'm still trying to process it. From the yelling to the whistle, it was definitely one to remember." Brooke turned toward the window. Any other day, she'd be laughing with Dan about what they'd just experienced.

"What did Emma say when you asked her about that?" Dan asked curiously.

"Apparently, she clerked for Southers, and there is some backstory about it—which is how she knew she would get Southers' appreciation and not be thrown out of her courtroom." Brooke turned from the window to face Dan.

"That makes sense. I would not have done that in her courtroom if I didn't know what the outcome was going to be." Dan shook his head. "Catch anything that was yelled?"

"Not really. It was much more Spanish than English. I got a couple of "this is your fault" comments, but my high school Spanish failed me again," Brooke said with a laugh. "This all adds to the question of what we are missing. Is it just the reactions we aren't used to?"

"I think that was more than just reactions we aren't used to. You and I have both been in courtrooms and responded to calls where voices and passions run high. This was something more. It happened so fast; I was a little stunned." Dan backed into his spot at the station as he spoke.

"You're right," Brooke said while unbuckling her seatbelt.

"At least we are done with crazy Aunt Maria." Dan got out of the car. And as Brooke stepped out, her gut was telling her he might not be quite right. Not this time.

* * *

June stood up from her desk when she saw Brooke and Dan walk in. "Detectives, you both clean up nicely!" It was impossible not to smile at this compliment. It felt like Mary Poppins herself was praising them.

"I am afraid I have some bad news, though, for Detective Hill." June walked around her desk. Judging by June's face, Brooke was dreading what she was about to say. "Greg Levine just called about five minutes ago. He asked that you call him back as soon as possible. My guess is that if you don't, he will just continue calling."

"Thanks, June," Brooke said, then she started walking to her office. Dan followed.

"Better you than me," he said as they walked into their office.

"Ha, no, partner. I am calling him back *with* you." Brooke replied with a grin as she picked up the phone without even unpacking her belongings. Dan gave her a look of dread. She put the call on speaker as it rang.

Dan glared at her. "What do you think he wants? To gloat?"

Brooke didn't get a chance to answer. Greg picked up his direct line right away. "Greg Levine."

"Hi Greg, it's Brooke Hill. You called?"

"Am I on speaker?" He must have been able to hear the slight echo.

"Yes, you are on speaker with my partner, Detective Dan Beal." Brooke rolled her eyes at Dan. "What can we do for you? I was surprised to see you in court today."

"The Halls asked me to come to represent them. That's the reason I am calling, actually." His smug tone once again snaked through the phone.

"Greg, this is Detective Beal. There is not our case at this point. We are no longer involved unless we are called, and even then, it needs to fall under our jurisdiction." Brooke nodded her head in approval. She liked that Dan was willing to go toe to toe with Greg right off the bat.

"I'm well aware of that, *Detective* Beal." Greg emphasized the word detective. "I want to know if you—both, I guess—would be willing to speak to my client?"

Brooke and Dan stared at each other. "Are you speaking about Matt Hall?" Brooke asked.

"Yes." Greg's answer was clipped.

Dan mouthed to Brooke, "What do you think he wants?"

"You are going to have to give us a little more than a one-word answer if you expect us to meet with him. Like my partner said, we are no longer involved." Brooke was losing patience with Greg Levine.

"I think we can all agree that today's antics in court were a spectacle. My client would like to speak to both of you about the possibility of pressing charges against his soon-to-be ex-wife Catalina Hall." The attorney's tone had turned matter of fact, and a tingle went down Brooke's spine.

"What do you mean press charges? What don't we know about, Greg?"

"Just that everything she accused him of is what she has done to him. And he has proof—actual proof. After the court proceedings today and the theatrics we witnessed, I instructed him to go down to the second floor and get a protective order. I heard from him right before I called you. He received one for two weeks . . . not forty-eight hours." Again, his smug tone came through as he spoke, and Brooke's stomach turned.

Dan leaned back in his chair, causing a creaking noise, and Brooke stared up at the ceiling. "Are you both still there?" the attorney asked.

"Yes," Dan and Brooke said in unison.

"Please have Matt reach out to us about coming in," Brooke finally said.

"Will do. Thank you." Greg hung up.

"Well," Dan said, straightening up in his chair. "What the heck?"

"I know," Brooke said. "That was unexpected. What do you think?"

"I can't tell if this is genuine or—" Dan broke off.

"Or something underhanded," Brooke finished his sentence.

"Guess we aren't quite done." Dan looked down at his phone and smiled. "Kat's got a doctor's appointment this afternoon. I had already taken leave for it. Do you mind?"

Brooke smiled at him. "Dan, even though you call me boss, I'm not. Go. I'll get a ride home from someone or get an Uber."

"Any chance I can interest you in coming over for dinner tomorrow? It's loud and crazy, but it would serve as a good distraction for whatever is taking space in your mind." Dan looked down at his phone.

"Kat tell you to invite me or is she reminding you that you need to leave?" Brooke asked.

"Both, actually. See you tomorrow?" Dan got up to leave and looked at Brooke, waiting for an answer. "Come on, Brooke, one hour of distraction will be good for you. And all the germs are gone."

Brooke offered the truest smile she'd felt in a long time. "What time?"

"Kat said six. And Brooke, don't wear anything nice, unless of course you want to add glitter to it."

CHAPTER 23

rooke sat in silence for a moment after Dan left the office. Dinner at the Dan and Kat's would be a good distraction from the deafening noise of her and Nick's relationship that currently filled her mind. Brooke checked her phone again. Silence. She pulled up their previous messages and began to type, and then quickly deleted it. Do I even really want to talk to him right now? The answer was no. He had treated her poorly over the past few days. Their last conversation began to replay in her mind and Brooke found herself increasingly getting angry. Angry at the way he had treated her and angry at herself for allowing this to happen. Angry that she felt so vulnerable and weak.... crying and crying again. Brooke opened her phone again to type out a message to Nick, this time determined to send. She started to type out a text telling him to not bother to contact her after he felt he had enough space when an unexpected text came through.

Sorry I missed you after court, let me know when you want to leave that stupid boyfriend at home and grab a drink. It was Brian. Brooke stared at her phone. *Maybe the feelings were one-sided when it came to Emma.*

Brooke quickly typed out a response before thinking, *tonight? Freddie's @ 7?* She sat back in her office chair and crossed her arms. *I am not doing anything wrong*, she said over and over again in her brain.

Brooke leaned forward as she saw the three dots appear on her screen indicating Brian was responding. *Meet u there.* Meeting Brian at Freddie's shifted Brooke's focus from her problems with Nick, to seeing Brian. *I'll wait till I have a clearer mind to deal with Nick*, Brooke thought. "Not sure how drinks with Brian will solve that," she muttered to herself as she flung her bag over her shoulder and headed out of her office to bum a ride from one of her fellow officers.

* * *

Freddie's was busy for a Thursday night and Brooke had to wait few minutes to just get in the bar. She stood on her tip toes to look for Brian. He had texted while she was still driving that he had just gotten there. She felt a strong hand on her back, "Hey."

Brooke jumped a little and turned. Brian. *God he's goodlooking.* He still had half his suit on from the day in court. He lost the jacket and tie, just white button-down shirt with the sleeves rolled up and the navy suit pants. "I saw you when you walked in. I called you and texted you to look to your left."

Brooke felt her back pocket and then immediately face palmed. "I left my phone in the car apparently."

"Do you need to go get it?" Brian asked as they both looked outside at the increasingly long line to get in.

"I'll survive. I need a drink more." Right on cue as Brooke stopped talking Violet appeared. She was dressed in a pink sparkle dress and her violet wig was done up in a beehive.

Violet air kissed Brooke on both cheeks. "Hello, love you want your usual?" She turned to Brian. "Well hello handsome, I see we have upgraded." She winked at Brooke.

Brooke rolled her eyes. "Vi anywhere to sit? It's packed for a Thursday."

"Karaoke night. Nothing the heteros love more than drag karaoke. There are some seats at the far end of the bar." Violet pointed in the direction of the end of the bar and was off before taking Brian's order.

Brian and Brooke made their way through the crowd to the end of the bar like Violet suggested. Brian pulled out Brooke's red linoleum bar stool out for her, she shot Brian a quizzical look. "My mom raised me right," he said smoothly in her ear.

Violet reappeared to officially take their drink orders, and before they could even finish exchanging pleasantries, she plopped two beers down and a basket of French fries on the house.

"Cheers," Brian held his beer on an angle to clink it with Brooke.

"Cheers, thanks for the invite out." Brooke clinked her bottle against his.

Brian smirked. "I think you were the one who asked me out."

Brooke nodded, "You're right, I did. I figured you would have already had plans though. Maybe with Emma?" Brooke was facing forward but gave Brian a side eye as she spoke, curious if her suspicions were correct.

"Subtle." Brian took a swig of his beer. "I'm well aware that everyone thinks Emma has a thing for me."

Brooke swung her body towards him in a dramatic fashion. "Do you think she does? Do you have a thing for her?"

Brian laughed. "You know for someone with a boyfriend you are asking a lot of questions about how I feel about a woman I work with."

Brooke put her head down. "Yea well that isn't going so well at the moment."

"Oh, I figured." Brian took a sip of his beer. "If you two were still all lovey dovey I doubt I would be the one sitting here next to you." Brian leaned his head towards Brooke and looked her in the eye. "Yes, I do think she has a thing for me, and no the feeling is not mutual. There is only one woman I am interested in; just hope she isn't using me to make her boyfriend mad."

Brooke put her hand on top of his. "I'm not, I genuinely wanted to see you."

Brian leaned closer and whispered in Brooke's ear, "who said I was talking about you?" The two of them began to laugh, the type of laugh that makes others stare and wonder what was so funny.

Their conversation continued alternating between serious and laughter. Before Brooke knew it, it was after midnight. "Good god, its 12:15." Brooke said as she looked at her red Apple Watch. "I've got to get going."

Brian threw a bunch of cash on the bar and turned to stand up. "Ready when you are."

"Thank you, you didn't need to pay." Brooke stood; she was so close to Brian she could feel his breath. As Brooke took a deep breath the smell of his sandalwood cologne enveloped her nostrils.

Brian grabbed her right hand and kissed it, "Happy too."

They walked out of the bar and Brian continued to walk alongside Brooke to the parking lot. "Did you park in this lot too?"

"No, I parked along the street." Brian motioned behind them. Brooke began to open her mouth to speak as they approached her car, but Brian cut her off. "I told you; my mom raised me right. I'm walking you to your car."

"And here I thought it was because you wanted to kiss me," Maybe it was the fighting with Nick, maybe it was all the beer that spurred Brooke on to encourage Brian in this way. She felt a pang of guilt, but quickly pushed it away, as Brian took a step closer to her.

Brian put both of his hands on her face. They were

looking deep in each other's eyes unable to speak, when they were interrupted by the sound of cellphone. Brooke turned and saw her phone ringing right where she left it, in the holder.

A picture of Brooke and Jacs from when they were in elementary school displayed across the screen. It was their first picture together trick-or-treating, Brooke was a ballerina and Jacs was a witch, complete with green face paint. Brooke turned to Brian, "I'll call her back." As Brian leaned in for a kiss, Brooke's phone went off again. Jacs.

"You should get that." Brian took a step back and gave Brooke a side smile. Brooke unlocked her car and grabbed the phone just in time before it hit voicemail. As soon as the call connected Jacs began to speak, not giving Brooke anytime to say hello.

"Pickle."

CHAPTER 24

Pickle was their safe word, the word they used from the time they were eight years old anytime either of them were in trouble. And trouble ranged from failing a test to the fateful night in college when Jacs ended up in the back of a police car for stealing a bottle of tequila from a fraternity party.

"Where are you?" Brooke asked looking at Brian, she could not hide her worry.

"My house. Get here now." Jacs was very matter of fact.

"I'll be there in five." They both hung up without saying goodbye.

Brooke looked up at Brian. She started to speak, but he stopped her. "Go. There is no pressure here, we can figure what this all means later."

"I'll text you later." She said as she got into her car.

Brian was still standing there as Brooke started her car. He knocked on the window indicating for her to roll the window down. As she did, he stuck his head through the open window and kissed Brooke's cheek. "She's fine you know that right? Who in their right mind would mess with Jacs."

* * *

"Air mattress is married," Jacs said as she opened the door to her apartment for Brooke. The nighttime guard Stanley waved Brooke through. He was seated at the front desk in front of several cameras that monitored the apartment complex. Even if Jacs hadn't called down to say she was coming Stanley wouldn't have thought twice about letting her go. They were on first name bases since the time four years ago when Jacs and Brooke locked themselves out of Jacs's apartment after a night out.

"Huh?" Brooke took a step into the apartment. Jacs had gone for minimalist ivory décor in her small one-bedroom home.

"Air mattress... is... married..." Jacs said this a little slower this time for Brooke. Brooke stared at her. Jacs was dressed in her signature color, black, black turtleneck and black skinny cropped pants. The only pops of color were the matching red nail polish on her fingers and toes. Her hair was down with a soft wave to it.

"Ok," Brooke put her hand on her arm. "Explains the no furniture at his place, I guess. I didn't think this was serious though?"

"It's not, but I'm no a homewrecker," Jacs tilted her head towards the bathroom. "That's not all."

Brooke looked from the bathroom that was just to their left and to Jacs. The door was shut. "Is he still here?"

"He won't leave," Jacs and Brooke stared at each other for a moment.

Jacs took a deep breath. "He came over tonight, we were sitting on the couch and his phone rang. He quickly looked at it and put it away, but not quick enough. Caller ID said wifey. You can imagine how I reacted." Both heard water turn on in the bathroom and instinctively looked before Jacs continued. "I told him to get out, he wanted to try and talk his way of it. I went towards the door; he grabbed my arm and... I punched him."

Brooke closed her eyes for a moment and then opened them. Jacs was staring at her blankly. "Where did you punch him Jacs?"

"Nose. He instantly started to bleed and went to the bathroom, and now every time I bang on the door, he tells me to go away. I can't get him to leave." They both turned again at the sound of a man coughing.

"He won't leave?" Brooke asked Jacs.

"Nope, the most I can get out of him is that I broke his nose." Jacs crossed her arms.

"Pickle." Brooke said loudly under her breath. "Ok." Brooke walked towards the bathroom door with Jacs behind her. She raised her hand to knock. "Wait, what is his actual name?"

"Russell Cotter." Jacs reached around Brooke and banged on the door.

"Go away," a deep man's voice answered from the other side of the door.

"This is Detective Hill with FCPD. Mr. Cotter you have one minute to get your belongs and leave Ms. Nissler's apartment." Silence followed Brooke's statement and then the lock on the door clicked. Russell Cotter opened the door. His nose was deeply swollen and already turning black and blue. His blue dress shirt was stained with blood.

"I want to press assault charges." He stared down Jacs. His short brown hair was disheveled.

"Ok. We can go down to the station and I can take your statement, and then I can call your wife and let her know why you are at the station pressing charges at this hour." Brooke was hoping that this statement wouldn't backfire. While deserving, Jacs did assault him and there was no plausible reason to call his wife.

Russell looked from Jacs to Brooke, pushed between them, walked towards through the hallway and slammed Jacs apartment door shut.

Jacs immediately picked up her phone and called the front desk. "Hey Stanley, it's Jacqueline Nissler in 609, can you please put into the system that Russell Cotter is not on my visitor list anymore? Thank you!"

"I can really pick'em," Jacs was shaking her head.

"I mean seriously Jacs," Brooke was laughing. "You find out the guy you are seeing is married, break his nose, and then he refuses to leave."

Jacs playfully hit Brooke's arm. "Only me."

"Only you. I need a drink after that." Brooke headed down the hall towards the kitchen.

"Oh my god same, I have vodka or wine." Jacs was in her small living room holding up a bottle of each.

"Vodka, and I am staying over. I've already decided I am taking off tomorrow" Brooke sat down in Jacs over-sized ivory couch. Jacs poured vodka into two glasses and handed one to Brooke.

Jacs sat down on the other matching couch. "Same. Where were you tonight? I called you about 40 times before you picked up."

Brooke took a sip of her vodka. "Almost kissing Brian Keenan." Brooke looked up from her drink to Jacs's shocked face.

It was a full minute before Jacs said a word. "Spill."

"I saw him in court this morning and then he texted earlier tonight and said let's grab a drink soon and I said how's tonight." Brooke took another sip, Jacs again was shocked. "I know, I know I said it because I am mad at Nick, I know I went because I am mad at Nick, and I know I almost kissed him because I am mad at Nick. None of this is an excuse for almost kissing someone who is not my boyfriend. Trust me I feel guilty enough, I'm just pushing those feelings way down at the moment." Brooke raised her glass, "vodka is helping with that."

Jacs was expressionless staring at Brooke.

"What?" Brooke was confused. She expected something other than a blank stare. Maybe a lecture about almost cheating on her boyfriend who she had waited years to be with?

"Why is it an almost kiss and not a kiss kiss?" Jacs was still expressionless as she took a sip of her drink.

"I'm confused, I thought you would lecture me about wanting to kiss someone other than Nick."

Jacs came over the sit next to Brooke. "We have enough people to judge us, we don't need to do it to each other. I might not like every decision you make, and as I just demonstrated you don't like all my decisions, but I would never lecture or judge you. You know that. Besides I don't really feel like I am in a position to say anything after what you just witnessed."

"Well damn now I wish I had." Both women laughed at this.

"When are you going to address the elephant in the room then?" Brooke knew exactly what Jacs was asking. What was she going to do about Nick. Not just with the almost kiss, but with the fighting and the obvious sneaking around. Brooke leaned her head back on Jacs's sofa and closed her eyes. As her thoughts danced from Nick to Brian sleep began to come. Through consciousness Brooke felt Jacs put a blanket on her and turn off the lights.

CHAPTER 25

After a somewhat restful night Brooke headed home early in the morning. She texted Dan and told him that she would not be in today but would be there for dinner that evening. Still no communication from Nick, which relieved Brooke a little now. No communication meant she did not need to deal with anything more now. Brooke did have a string of texts from Brian ranging from hoping she had a good day, to reminiscing about almost kissing her. This gave Brooke butterflies, the good kind. Which then lead to feelings of guilt...

Brooke spent the day straightening up her house and laundry, anything to take her mind off the love triangle she had accidently created. Before she knew it, she was dressed in a glitter proof outfit, jeans and a green t-shirt, both of which she didn't care if Dan's girls redecorated.

Dan and Kat Beal's house was a picturesque blue and white bungalow from the 1920s. Set on a quiet street only a few minutes from the station, their house was easy to pick out. A sea of pink big wheels and bikes lay across the front yard, with a red minivan parked in the driveway sporting stick people of each member of their family, including two dogs, on the back windshield. Brooke parked behind the van and maneuvered around a string of Barbies lining the walkway. The front door was left open, only a screen door closed. Brooke knocked, and a little tow-haired girl with curls, about five years old, came bopping down the stairs.

"Brooke!" It was Abby, Dan and Kat's oldest. "I'm so happy you're here for spaghetti night!" She'd pronounced it *ba-sghetti.* Brooke gave the girl a big hug.

"Girlfriend, I told you that you are not allowed to open the door for anyone," Kat said, rounding the corner and holding their youngest, Bridget. Pregnancy suited her well; her natural glow was enhanced, and her rosy cheeks looked like she'd expertly applied blush.

"Sorry, Mommy!" and Abby was off running into the kitchen.

"Hi, Brooke. You look great." Kat gave Brooke a one-armed side hug.

"Thank you, and so do you. How are you feeling?" Brooke asked as she followed Kat into the small kitchen. Dan was manning the stove.

"Big," Kat said with a laugh. "Can I get you some wine?"

"I'm good, thanks. Can I help?" Brooke approached Dan as she spoke.

"My spaghetti is world-renowned, boss. You just sit down and relax the best you can." Dan had just stopped talking when two golden retrievers came tumbling in from the back door. Ellie, their precocious three-year-old, walked in proudly after them. She had mud on her face that matched the mud on the dogs' paws. *The precious tomboy*, Brooke thought.

"I took Baxter and Bailey out all by myself!" She sat down and took a sip of chocolate milk. It took her half a second to realize Brooke was sitting there too. "Brookie!" She ran and gave her a hug. "Daddy, can we have Shirley Temples in fancy glasses tonight? Brookie, you have to have one!"

"Of course, sweetheart. How about we make them?" Brooke said with a hug to Ellie.

Armed with Shirley Temples in plastic champagne glasses, they all sat down at the round kitchen table. It took the kids all of five minutes to eat their food, and then they were ushered off by Kat to watch the latest Disney movie in the sunken family room.

Brooke relaxed into her chair. "Thank you, Dan. You were right. This is exactly what I needed." Dan clinked his beer against her Shirley Temple.

"Okay, what are we talking about first: Nick or the case?" Kat came back from the family room and sat next to Dan, draping one arm around him.

Brooke smiled. "I think I would rather talk about the case and leave Nick alone."

Kat and Dan looked at each other. "Of course. Just know we are here for you." Kat reached a hand for Brooke.

"That obvious that I need a 'we are here for you' talk?" Brooke looked at Kat and squeezed her hand.

"I think it is more that we both know you and Nick are not acting normal, and neither of you is talking about it. Since he is not answering me . . ." Dan trailed off.

"We always liked you better, anyway." Kat winked at Brooke.

Brooke knew looking at her two friends that she was going to have to say something to satisfy their worrying. "I'm not going to lie about being okay. Honestly, I don't understand what is going on. But I will be okay."

"Good thing your sister is the actor and not you," Kat said, and the three of them laughed.

"Did Dan tell you about court yesterday?" Brooke hoped to change the subject.

"The whistle heard round the world. That was a ballsy move." Kat whistled as she said this.

"That was used to end a most epic screaming match." Brooke took a sip of her Shirley Temple. She stared at the vibrant red color as she placed her glass down on the table.

"Then the plot twist phone call that afternoon," Dan chimed in.

"I still don't know what to make of that call." Brooke rubbed her forehead, thinking of the yesterday's events.

"I was thinking about that. I think we should follow Catalina." Dan took a sip of his beer. "Unofficially."

Kat looked worried. Brooke stepped in. "What are you plotting, Beal?"

"I propose that I follow her—again, unofficially—for

twenty-four hours. Depending on what I find, we go to the Lieutenant." Dan seemed overly confident.

"You talked to the Lieutenant already, didn't you?" Brooke eyed Dan.

He deflected with another sip of his beer before meeting Brooke's stare. "Maybe."

Kat let out a long sigh. "And when is this happening?"

"Tomorrow night. Your parents are coming into town tomorrow morning." Dan looked at Kat. His wife started to protest, but he cut her off with a gift. "They are bringing you a cheesesteak."

Kat closed her mouth and looked from Dan to Brooke. "I can't turn down an authentic cheesesteak. Throw in two, and you can do this all week."

The apprehension was growing across Brooke's face giving her feelings away.

"Are you pissed that I talked to the Lieutenant without you?" Dan looked worried now.

"Not at all. I just feel like I should be with you, doing this with you. I just don't know if it's a good idea." Brooke felt concern creep in, something in her soul. She didn't trust Catalina or her aunt and had a bad feeling about all of it.

"It's a weekend. You aren't on duty, and I volunteered to do this. Look, I am either going to see something good and call you immediately or be bored stiff for twenty-four hours." Dan stood up to clear the table. As if on cue, three little blonde girls came running back into the kitchen.

"Okay, you three, time to get ready for bed. Give hugs to Brooke before we head up," Kat said above all the giggling.

Brooke offered the munchkins a big group hug and promised to bring lots of glitter next time she visited. Then she turned to give Kat a hug, "promise to call if she needed anything."

"Ditto," Kat said with a grin.

Brooke grabbed a few plates and brought them over to the sink. "Thank you, Dan, I needed this."

"You are always welcome. And if you ever want to experience these precious daughters of ours alone, you can absolutely take them." Dan turned from the sink to face her. His smile was infectious.

Brooke laughed. "Yeah, don't bet on it. I'm going to head home. Thank you again." She saw Dan dry his hands so he could walk her out. She put up her hand. "Don't. It's totally fine. I can easily walk to the front door myself."

He nodded. "See you later, boss."

Brooke got into her car but paused before turning it on. She felt better having spent the night away from the station and her home. Reflecting on the laughter, the Shirley Temples, the mud on paws and faces, and the innocence, she realized more and more that she wanted what Dan and Kat had. But did she want it with Nick or Brian?

Brooke looked down at her phone. A goodnight text from Brian awaited reading, still more silence from Nick.

CHAPTER 26

D inner at Kat and Dan's was the distraction Brooke needed for a goodnight sleep. She could have slept even longer but was awakened by her phone ringing on its charger on the bedside table.

Brooke jolted upright with the noise. Her heart skipped, thinking it was Nick, and then sank when she saw it was Aunt T.

"Hi, Aunt T," Brooke said groggily.

"I'm so sorry—did I wake you?" Aunt T seemed genuinely surprised that Brooke had been still asleep. Brooke pulled back the phone to check the time. It was 9:00 a.m.

"It's fine. I need to wake up. What's up?" Brooke fumbled with the array of water bottles and books on her nightstand, looking for her glasses.

"Do you want to go for a run this morning? It is beautiful out. We can grab brunch at one of those great places overlooking the water." Aunt T said with a hopeful tone.

Brooke didn't hesitate. "Yes, absolutely!"

"Great! See you at our normal meetup spot in about an hour."

Brooke agreed, and Aunt T hung up. Brooke stretched

her arms and legs into a full body stretch, reaching across the bed as she formed an *X* with her body.

* * *

Brooke pulled her car into a parking spot at Gravelly Point Park. The park was right next to the international airport, so it was often crowded with airplane enthusiasts. Aunt T loved to run at the park and found watching the planes a serene bonus to the grueling exercise.

Brooke spotted Aunt T right away; she was stretching by a group of people getting ready for an ultimate frisbee game. Being dressed all in black made her red-framed glasses stand out even more.

Aunt T looked up as Brooke approached. "Hi, love," she said as she hugged Brooke. "Do you need to stretch or are you good to go?"

"I'm good. Let's just get going," Brooke replied, looking off at the distance. She was again thinking about Nick. She had silenced his alerts, hoping that would make her stop checking her phone as much, but it'd had the opposite effect. She found herself checking it even more.

"Do you want to talk about whatever is bothering you or just run?" Aunt T had placed her hand on Brooke's arm, sensing something wasn't quite right.

"I think I need to clear my head first if that is okay with you." Brooke turned to face Aunt T.

"Of course, I'm here when and if you want to talk about

anything in particular," Aunt T said. "Let's run this way." She pointed away from the airport.

Brooke knew she could clear her thoughts once she began running with Aunt T. They started the jog in silence, but once she found her stride, she became willing to talk. Avoiding anything serious, Brooke and Aunt T discussed making a trip up to New York City to see Cassie.

The two women slowed down as they approached their favorite coffee shop.

"Do you want to stop here or keep going for brunch?" Aunt T was a half-step ahead of Brooke.

Brooke slowed to a stop. "Let's just grab a coffee here and see how we feel."

"Sounds like a plan. I'll run in. Want the usual?" Aunt T turned to ask Brooke.

"Yes, please—and a water." Brooke headed to a near-by bench to sit. As Aunt T walked into the shop, Brooke once again checked her phone. Nothing from Nick. A text from Brian asking if she was free for dinner appeared. She smiled.

"Excuse me, are you Brooke? Brooke Hill?" A petite blonde woman stood before her. She wore yoga clothes, with a purple mat slung over her shoulder.

"Yes," Brooke answered. "I'm sorry, do I know you?" The woman looked familiar, but she couldn't place her. *Did I go to high school with her? College?* They looked to be about the same age.

"I don't think we've ever officially met. I'm Liv, Liv

Black." The name registered, and recognition spread across Brooke's face.

"As in—" Brooke began.

"As in Nick's ex." Liv finished her sentence. She felt instantly nervous as to why Live picked now to approach her, the new sweat on her palms not from the run.

"Sorry . . . I'm just surprised and honestly confused to be meeting you now," Brooke managed to get out.

"I understand. I was walking out of the yoga studio, and I spotted you. I remember your photo from Nick's apartment." Liv said. "I wasn't sure if I should come over or not." She looked at her feet.

"Um, no, it's fine." Brooke was getting more and more confused by this interaction, and more nervous.

"I just wanted to apologize." Liv's feet shuffled beneath her.

"I'm sorry—I don't follow. Apologize for what?" A warning signal went off in her brain.

Liv's face went white. "Oh my god. He didn't tell you yet."

"Tell me what?" Brooke asked with urgency.

"I'm so sorry. I shouldn't be the one to tell you." Liv was shaking her head.

"Tell me *what?*" Brooke stood up and realized she towered over the young woman, so she took a step back to catch her breath.

"I have to go." Liv turned to leave. "You should talk to Nick. He really needs to be the one to tell you this."

Brooke grabbed Liv's arm. "Liv, what is it?"

Liv's face flashed fear, but instead of yelling out, she took a deep breath and looked into Brooke's eyes. Silence fell between them, and Brooke let go of her arm.

"Liv, I am begging you. Please tell me whatever it is that you thought I knew." Brooke was still close enough to the woman that she could feel her breath.

"Brooke, I'm so sorry," Liv said as she looked down again. "I never thought this would happen, and we never meant to hurt anyone. We are honestly just trying to navigate this."

Brooke opened her mouth to speak again, but Liv cut her off. "I'm pregnant." As Liv looked down at her stomach, Brooke looked down, too, and saw the unmistakable pooch of a baby bump.

CHAPTER 27

"**W**ait . . . what?" Brooke stepped back. She felt instantly light-headed and glanced toward the bench she'd been sitting on, but her legs wouldn't move.

"I'm so sorry. I shouldn't have even come over." Liv was tearing up, her green eyes looking glassy.

"You're pregnant?" Brooke couldn't believe the words coming out of her mouth.

"I really thought Nick had told you. I am so sorry. I really need to go." Liv turned the other way to retreat.

Brooke shook her head and reached for her. "No, wait. You can't go. You can't tell me this and then just leave." She couldn't help it; the volume of her voice rose. She had so many questions rushing through her mind. "When did you tell Nick? How far along are you?"

"Brooke, look I am so sorry to have come over here, to have told you all this. I just felt so bad, and selfishly, I wanted to apologize. But you really need to talk to Nick. I mean it; I have to go." Liv had fully turned now.

"Wait! Please!" Brooke felt a lump in her throat start to form, her own tears on the verge of spilling. She softened her voice. "Liv, please."

Liv turned around to face Brooke. She took a deep breath in. "I'm about four months along."

Brooke looked down to keep from crying. That timing ... the realization that Nick had cheated on her sunk in. Her cheeks grew hot with shame.

"I know this doesn't matter, but it was a onetime thing, and this was obviously not the plan. I had started a new relationship, too, when I found out." Liv was looking everywhere but at Brooke.

"When did you tell Nick?" Brooke's voice cracked through a growing sob.

"I wanted to wait to tell him. I needed time to process it all before I spoke to him. I've tried him a few times off and on for a few weeks, he finally picked up a few days ago, early one morning."

It all came together now. The phone calls, the stress, the not wanting to talk about it yet. He knew this would destroy everything. The tears rushed down Brooke's face.

Liv backed up. "I have to go. For what it's worth, Brooke, I am truly sorry." Liv turned and walked away.

Brooke couldn't move. She was frozen with the weight of the news Liv had just broken. The tears still flowed down her cheeks as Aunt T approached. Her aunt just stood next to Brooke, not saying a word.

"How much of that did you hear?" Brooke asked between sobs.

"Enough." Aunt T handed Brooke her coffee. "I heard enough." She put her now free arm around Brooke.

They stood outside the coffee shop for what seemed

like hours rather than minutes. The ringing of Brooke's phone brought her back to the present. She wiped her face and pulled out her phone from the side pocket of her running pants. *Nick.*

"You don't have to answer it," Aunt T said, looking at Brooke's phone. "But you will have to deal with this eventually."

The ringing stopped momentarily before it began again. Brooke looked up to the sky, breathed in, said a silent prayer to give her strength for what was coming next. "Hello?"

"Brooke—I . . ." Nick started. She could picture him pacing his small apartment, running his fingers through his hair.

"Where are you?" Brooke asked, hoping she sounded steadier than she felt.

"I'm at my apartment. But Brooke—"

Brooke cut him off. "I'll be there in ten minutes." She hung up, not giving him a chance to talk. She turned toward Aunt T.

"I just called for an Uber, quicker to take one than run back to your car. Nick was in my saved addresses from when I met you both there for drinks." She patted Brooke's arm.

"Thank you, Aunt T." Brooke hugged her aunt, grateful that she was standing next to her right now.

"Be strong. You know how you deserve to be treated. Don't stand for anything less." Aunt T whispered in her ear.

* * *

Brooke was at Nick's apartment in less than ten minutes. Her Uber had been prompt and there was little traffic. Nick lived in an apartment building not far from the heart of Old Town Alexandria. It was an older brick building with just two stories. He was on the first level, around the back of the building. Brooke walked through the courtyard and approached his door. She was about to knock when Nick opened it.

"Hi." He was dressed in pajama bottoms and an old Police Academy T-shirt.

"Hi." Brooke knew how upset she looked. She'd glanced at her reflection in the mirror on the ride over. Her face was red and blotchy, her eyes swollen.

She walked past him as he held open the door and stood in his small foyer. "Do you want to sit down? Something to drink?" He was being very polite. Nick was clearly nervous, unsure of how this was going to go.

"No, I'd rather stand." Brooke couldn't make eye contact with him.

"Brooke—" Nick began.

She put her hand up. She wasn't in the mood to play games or stall. "So, I assume Liv called you. I won't be nagging you to tell me what is going on anymore. You know, since she let me know about the *baby*." Brooke knew her words were cruel, but her shock was wearing off, and anger was setting in.

"I don't know what to say." Nick stared at her, caught in his deceitfulness.

"There's a baby? When were you going to drop that bomb?" Brooke asked, again refusing to divert her gaze.

Nick sighed. "Brooke, I'd just found out I am going to be a dad. I needed to process it on that level first—then figure out how to tell you." He reached out his hand to touch her arm. She took a giant step back so he couldn't reach her. It was meant to be an obvious sign to him— there'd be no forgetting.

"You mean, figure out how to lie some more to me?" Brooke didn't care how mean she was being. This entire situation hurt, deeply.

"I deserve that." Nick looked down again.

Brooke didn't want to hear anymore, she turned to walk out the door. She did not feel like she needed to address their relationship. As far as she was concerned, it was over. She never wanted anything to do with him, ever again.

"Brooke, wait." Nick took two steps forward to get between her and his front door. "I have no right to ask you to forgive me, or . . . especially, to do this with me. I am so sorry. I can't believe the pain that I am causing you right now." He ran his fingers through his hair. "You know, you and me, this is *it*. This was always my end game. My parents are so in love, to this day. And I've always wanted that, the way my dad looks at my mom. That is the way I feel about you."

Nick reached his hand to touch Brooke's face. His words had worked. This time, she let him. He continued, "I have no right to ask this, but I am going to. Can we talk in a few days? When the weight of what is happening has sunk in and the anger has subsided a bit?"

Brooke pulled away. It felt like too much of a concession. "I don't know. Right now, I don't want to talk to you. I don't want to see you. You are having a baby with another person. Not to mention, the way I found out...I can't even look at you now. I need to leave."

Brooke sidestepped Nick and reached for the door. But he grabbed her forearm. "Brooke, please." She was reminded of her grabbing Liv's arm and begging her to talk some more too.

"To quote you, 'You need to give me space.'" Brooke turned the front doorknob and walked out, determined not to look back.

CHAPTER 28

Brooke walked a few blocks to clear her head then called another Uber to go home. Once there she walked directly to her bedroom. She turned on her TV for background noise, lay on her bed, and pulled the covers over her head, desperately trying to will herself to sleep, to erase the memory of the morning.

Sleep came and went, so Brooke remained in a hypnagogic state. *This was just a bad dream*, she thought. *At any moment, I will wake up, and everything will be as it was. This can't be happening.* But it was happening, and when that reality came and went, so did the tears.

She was occasionally startled awake by her phone or a loud noise on her TV. After a few hours, Brooke thought she had heard voices and footsteps in her house. Any desire to see who was calling or if someone was, in fact, inside her house just wasn't there. She didn't care. *Nick is having a baby with Liv.* Those thoughts kept racing through her head. This was now her reality.

Liv. Liv standing in front of her with her baby bump. Nick's baby. She was having Nick's baby. Brooke wanted to hate her, and she did, partly, but the look on her face.

The look on Liv's face when she realized she was the one having to tell Brooke she was pregnant was one of deep remorse. But she was having Nick's *baby*. Sleep came again.

"I don't know, this reminds me more of the scene in *Crazy Rich Asians*. You know, right after the wedding when she finds out they dug into her past."

"No, I'm telling you it's from the *Sex and the City* movie when Big leaves Carrie at the altar. They go to Mexico, and she won't get out of bed. She's acting more like Carrie."

Brooke smiled. The unmistakable voices of her best friend and sister filled her bedroom. She peeled her flowered bedspread off her head and sat up. Her favorite people were standing in the doorway. "What's the movie where the girl falls madly in love with one of her closest friends, only to find out that he cheated on her and got another girl pregnant?" Brooke began to cry.

Jacs and Cassie rushed across the hardwoods and enveloped her in a group hug. No words were exchanged for several minutes while they held onto each other tightly.

Finally, Brooke pulled away. "Thank you both for being here."

Cassie reached for a tissue and handed it to Brooke. Jacs gave Cassie a look and handed Brooke the entire box.

"Aunt T called me yesterday after you got into the Uber. I called Jacs right away, and we came as soon as we could." Cassie rested her hand on her leg.

"Yesterday?" Brooke looked from Cassie to Jacs. "What time is it? Is it Sunday?"

"It's about eleven in the morning, yes—Sunday. You've been in bed for almost twenty-four hours." Jacs put her hand on Brooke's other leg. Brooke looked down. She was still in her running clothes.

"I didn't realize it had already been a whole day. I just wanted to turn the world off for a little bit." Brooke looked down at the crumbled-up tissue in her hand.

"That's understandable." Cassie gave her a sympathetic look.

Brooke grabbed another tissue and blew her nose. "I need to call Aunt T. I'm sure she is worried."

"No need. She and Carol were just here. They stocked the kitchen with all your favorite foods, and Carol made about seven dishes that are in your fridge and freezer," Cassie said with a laugh.

"They supplied the food, and we brought the vodka." Jacs smiled. "How about you take a long, hot shower, and we get you something to eat?"

Brooke sighed. "Do I look as bad as I feel?"

"Worse—and you smell." Jacs laughed as Brooke threw one of the crumbled tissues at her.

"Seriously, go shower. We will clean up all the tissues, wash your sheets and clothes, and get you something to eat. I'll go turn on your shower." Cassie moved to get up, but Brooke grabbed her hand.

"Thank you. I want to say you didn't need to come, but the truth is I need you. I need you both." Brooke was choking back tears.

"And that is exactly why we are here," Jacs said as she grabbed Brooke for a side hug on the edge of her bed.

* * *

After a long shower and donning some clean clothes, Brooke was starting to feel more human. She checked her phone before she entered the kitchen. She had a slew of texts and calls from Jacs, Cassie, Aunt T, Carol, and even Benji. There was also one from Beal, saying he was starting his surveillance of Catalina. Nothing from Nick. Brooke sighed. She didn't want to hear from him, but she also wanted him to be gravelling. Brooke quickly typed out a text to Aunt T to let her know that she was alive. She knew Aunt T would be worried, even though she'd just been there.

Jacs and Cassie were waiting for her with a turkey and cheddar sandwich and a variety of drinks. "We weren't sure what you wanted, so we have water, coffee, vodka, and champagne." Cassie pointed to each cup.

"I don't know that champagne is appropriate for this occasion," Brooke said with a smirk aimed at Jacs.

Jacs leaned over to Brooke. "You don't need a reason to pop a bottle of champagne." She winked and flicked her hand.

Brooke laughed. "So true, but I think I will stick to a cup of coffee, water, and maybe some Advil."

"Coming right up." Cassie moved to grab the coffee and Advil.

"I just keep hoping this is a dream." Brooke took the coffee from Cassie and headed to her oversized navy-blue couch. She grabbed one of her yellow throw pillows to hold.

Jacs went to the corner and grabbed an ultra-soft white blanket and handed it to Brooke. "I would imagine that's completely normal. But, just like all bad dreams, you have to wake up and start living again. No matter how hard it is." Jacs sat on one side of Brooke, Cassie the other.

Brooke took a deep breath. "You're right. I have to keep living. I have to move on."

"Just to be clear, we aren't forgiving him, right?" Cassie looked from Brooke to Jacs.

Both women turned their heads in shock at Cassie. Cassie put her hands up in a surrender motion. "I am just clarifying."

"There is no way we could move past this." Brooke's blue eyes welled with tears again.

"Every day will get easier." Jacs went in for another side hug.

"I know. I know it will." Brooke leaned her head on Jacs's shoulder. "I can't help but feel guilty though too.."

Jacs cut her off, "Don't you dare compare almost kissing Brian to what Nick did."

Cassie looked from Brooke to Jacs to Brooke again. "Jacs already told me, we can dive into that one later, but she's right. Almost kissing Brian is nowhere close to what Nick did. Do you want to watch a movie, might be a good distraction? Maybe *Steel Magnolias?*" Cassie asked. It had been a family favorite for decades, originating with their mother and Aunt T. All the women in the family could recite nearly every line by heart.

"That sounds perfect." Brooke looked at her sister and smiled.

Brooke curled up on the couch, with Cassie on the floor next to her and Jacs in the oversized brown leather chair in the corner. It only took a few minutes for sleep to wash over Brooke once more.

CHAPTER 29

Brooke woke up to the glow of a beautiful dusk sky seeping through her living room windows. She looked around and found herself alone, but a sticky note was attached to her still full coffee mug.

Had to run home. Cassie is in the guest bedroom sleeping. She didn't get a lot of sleep last night. Text me when you wake up. Remember, no matter how bad the nightmare is, you have to wake up. You have to keep living. Love you lots and lots. —Jacs

Jacs was right. Brooke had to keep living. This was happening. This was reality. Brooke walked across her hardwood floors barefoot to the guestroom door. It was opened a crack. Brooke could see the sea of curly brown hair under the oversized white duvet cover. Not wanting to disturb Cassie and feeling guilty for the fact that she was most likely the reason Cassie didn't sleep last night, she crept into the kitchen. She cleaned up the few dishes that had not made their way into the dishwasher and opened the fridge to grab something to eat.

They weren't kidding. Her fridge had never been so full. Carol and Aunt T had fully stocked it with all her favorite foods, homemade meals, and even food from her childhood, like little Jello jars. She settled on a cherry-flavored one and headed back into her bedroom.

Jacs and Cassie had cleaned up the sea of tissues, washed her sheets, made her bed, and straightened up. Brooke said a silent prayer, thanking God for the two of them. She didn't realize how much she needed them till she'd seen them earlier that day.

Brooke surveyed her bedroom and noticed a pile of Nick's stuff in the corner. Jacs and Cassie must have tried to collect all the things they thought were his. Brooke looked around again and noticed that they had hidden the two photos she'd had out of her and Nick. She was grateful for this. She did not want to be reminded of happier times.

As she stared again at Nick's pile, her heart sank. A sweatshirt, a pair of pajama pants, a hat, and an iPhone charger. That was all that was left of her relationship with him. The one that was supposed to be the great love in her life—the forever one.

Jacs's voice rang out in her head. *You have to keep*

living. Brooke turned and headed out to her carport. She dug through her recycling bin and found an empty box that was still taped together. Bringing it back into her bedroom, she put all of the things that belonged to Nick into the box. Not wanting to stop for a moment, lest she ruminate too much and get weepy all over again, she grabbed her car keys and headed back out to the carport, not stopping to wonder how her car made it back to her house. She popped the trunk to her Camry and placed the box inside.

Shutting the trunk, she was startled to see Cassie standing there. "Jesus, Cassie, you scared the crap out of me!" Brooke shouted, clutching her heart.

"Sorry, I heard doors opening and shutting. I was coming to see what was going on, and I saw you standing by your car. You aren't going back over to Nick's, are you?" Cassie was still half-asleep as they spoke in the driveway, yawning and scratching her head of curls.

"No, definitely not. I saw the pile of Nick's stuff and I just—I just didn't want to have to look at it. I boxed it up and put it in my trunk. I can leave it by his car at the station one day next week or something." Brooke was looking off into the distance, trying not to cry.

"I'm sorry. We weren't exactly sure what you would want to do with his stuff. I mean, we wanted to burn everything, but it is really up to you." Cassie was becoming more herself as she woke up.

"I really appreciate you guys getting his stuff in a pile

and taking down the pictures . . . on top of everything else you have done over the past twenty-four hours." Brooke took two steps toward her sister and hugged her hard.

"You would do the same for me and for Jacs. Just let me know when you want to know where we hid the pictures." Cassie pulled back. "Jacs is on her way back and is going to pick up take-out. What are you in the mood for?"

Brooke's normal go-to of Chinese brought back a flood of memories of her last meal with Nick at the Nobles' house. She shook her head to get the thoughts out of her mind. "How about Indian?"

Cassie pulled out her phone to text Jacs. "Perfect. Oh, also, while you were asleep, Dan called a few times. I wouldn't normally pick up, but after the third time, I figured I better."

"Did he say anything?" Brooke asked.

"Just that you need to call him back." Cassie looked up as she slipped her phone in the back of her jeans pocket. "Sounded like he had just gotten some good gossip."

Brooke frowned.

"I meant about a case, not about anything else." Cassie realized she may have made a mistake using the word gossip.

"I'm sure it's that. I'll be back inside in a minute. I want to give him a call back." Brooke pulled out her phone from the side pocket of her navy sweatpants. She frowned when she saw she had no notifications from Nick.

Cassie picking up on this, stood a little closer to Brooke.

"Space at first is hard. Give yourself some grace, sis. Oh, and you should text Benji when you get a chance, he brought your car back" She squeezed Brooke's arm and headed up the driveway when she turned and smiled. "Oh, and you really should call Brian too, he may have also called..." She laughed to herself and headed inside.

Brooke smiled thinking about Brian, the first smile in the past 24 hours. She decided to call Dan first, he picked up instantly. "'Bout time there, boss," Dan said sarcastically.

"It's been a day . . . or two," Brooke said, her voice still a little shaky.

"You, okay?"

There was no way Dan wouldn't pick up that something was wrong from the sound of Brooke's voice. "Yes . . . no, but I don't want to focus on it." Brooke looked up at the sky, which was turning from dusk to dark. "Cassie said you had called, and she made it sound like you had something good to tell me."

"Oh, do I," Dan started. "I know it's Sunday night, but any chance you can meet me at the station? I'm about ten minutes from there."

"Sure. Assuming you found something while you were following Catalina? Are the tables turned, and she is now stalking Matt?" Brooke poked around to see what Dan had found out.

"Oh, there is a Hall involved—just not the one you think."

CHAPTER 30

After reassuring Jacs and Cassie she would not be long, Brooke drove to the station in silence. She needed the quiet to try to stop her mind from spinning. As she parked, she checked her phone. Silence. Nothing from Nick. He was respecting her boundary for space, which she was both happy and sad about.

Dan was seated at his desk, waiting for her. He had his feet propped up and was looking at his phone as she walked in.

"Hey," Dan said as Brooke walked in. Then a look of concern spread across his face.

"You, okay?" Dan said as Brooke maneuvered her way to her desk chair.

"That obvious?" Brooke knew her eyes were still swollen and her face still red and blotchy. She had on her old high school sweatshirt and sweatpants from her field hockey days. They were showing their age with the threadbare navy cotton fabric.

"No offense, boss, but you look like hell." Dan watched her as she took a seat.

"I feel that way too." She let out a sigh as she situated herself opposite him.

"Understandable," Dan nodded sympathetically. "I talked to Nick."

Brooke sighed again. "I figured you would at some point. Listen, I am not ready to talk about it, and I'm not sure I ever will want to."

Dan nodded, not knowing what to say.

"So, what did you find out from your very exciting stakeout?" Brooke asked, changing the subject.

"I prefer *tailing*—much more exciting." Dan, picking up on her need to change subjects, tried to lighten the mood as well. "Want to start guessing?"

"Her and Matt are secretly happily married and trying to work the system somehow? Or Aunt Maria is not her aunt but her girlfriend." Brooke knew that both were unlikely and was playing along. Secretly, though, she had a hunch about what might be happening.

"This is almost as good." Dan paused for dramatic effect. "Catalina is—

"Sneaking around with Andrew Hall." Brooke had an epiphany in the car ride to the station Nick's big secret had awakened something in her gut.

"You figured it out?" Dan was shocked she had beat him to his big revelation.

"Big secrets are going around apparently." The last word trailed off as Brooke continued. "So, sneaking around how?" Brooke asked, matching Dan's posture as she crossed her arms and leaned back in her chair.

"Glad you asked. I started following her on Saturday morning. Nothing unusual. She made a trip to the grocery store, came back. Then, that night, there was a man lurking in the shadows, dressed in all black with his hood up. I thought, *okay, here we go—she wasn't lying.* Then he pulled out his phone. I couldn't see what exactly he was doing, but the porch light went out. I again thought that maybe somehow Matt had electronic control of it. I had one hand on my door and another on my gun. I was ready. He approached the front door, and it opened. Catalina was standing there and then . . . she threw her arms around him and kissed him." Dan paused.

"I would have assumed it was Matt based on that," Brooke said.

"I did, but I didn't get a good look at his face, so I waited. All night—and all day. The door finally opened at four p.m. It was Catalina and the man. She gave him another throw-your-arms-around-you kiss, and he left." Again, Dan paused.

"And being the *expert tailer* you are, you got a clear look at his face?" Brooke asked.

"I did, and I took a photo." Dan handed her his cell phone. "I knew it wasn't Matt right away, but he does have a similar look. I did a quick Google search and found a picture of Drew Hall. That's definitely him, right?" Dan took his phone back and pulled up the picture of Drew Hall that he'd found. Brooke looked at it and then back to the photo Dan had.

"I would say so," Brooke said, again leaning back in her chair.

"What do we do with it?" Dan asked. "It's pretty scandalous."

"Agreed, but I don't know what we do with it. It's not right, but there is no law against cheating on your husband with his brother." Brooke just knew this new development was part of the mysterious piece they were missing. "Unless, of course, you are trying to manipulate the law to get your husband in trouble."

"I think this is the part of the puzzle we have been looking for." Dan was very satisfied with his discovery.

"I think we need to sit on it and figure out how to really connect this. We need more proof before we take it to the Lieutenant. Let's let it marinate and come back together in the morning." Brooke knew she was in no position to think clearly right then.

"I agree. I'm going to head out. I need to relieve Kat before she leaves me," Dan said with a laugh. As he got up to go, their office phone rang. Brooke motioned for him to go.

"Go, I'll answer it. On a Sunday night, probably a wrong number. If it is something we need to deal with now, I'll text you to come back." Brooke reached for the phone.

Sounds good. See you in the mornin'." Dan turned to leave.

"This is Detective Hill," Brooke said as she answered the phone.

"Detective Hill, I wasn't sure I would be able to catch you on a Sunday night."

Oh, God, why did I have to pick up? Brooke rubbed her temples where a headache was forming at the sound of Greg Levine's voice. "Greg, why are you calling me on a Sunday?"

"Taking a chance that you might be there," he said, as smug as ever. "Glad I did. It's like I have superpowers."

"What can I do for you? I was just about to head out." Brooke hated that she asked how she could help and hated even more that she did not just let the phone go to voicemail.

"Matt Hall is on his way over to the station" Greg said.

Brooke's interest was piqued now that she might have an upper hand after Dan's latest discovery. "I will be in at about eight tomorrow. I can meet with him—" Brooke started but was cut off.

"He's driving to the station as we speak. I told him that I would call first to make sure you were there." Greg was just assuming she would stick around, which irked her to no end.

"Greg, I can't. I have to get ho—" Again Greg Levine cut her off.

"Brooke, you are going to want to hear what he has to say."

CHAPTER 31

Matt Hall strolled into the station again looking like the All-American poster boy. His short blonde side part didn't have a hair out of place. He wore a faded gray American University sweatshirt and had dark jeans on. Brooke was waiting for him in the lobby, still seething that Greg Levine had manipulated the situation. Matt outstretched his hand to hers in greeting.

"Detective Hill, thank you so much for meeting me tonight," Matt said. He seemed sincerely appreciative.

"Let's talk in my office." Brooke led the way to her and Dan's office. She hadn't texted Dan to come back. She wanted to see what Matt had to say first, then she'd call him. Dan had willingly been on duty, with no sleep, for over twenty-four hours, so she figured it was her turn.

"You can sit at my partner's desk." Brooke saw Matt looking around for a place to sit and gestured toward Dan's chair.

"Thank you." Matt sat down, ran his fingers through his hair, and looked over at Brooke. That movement made her insides twist. It was Nick's trademark tic, and here was Matt, doing the same thing. She shook it off. *Priorities, Hill.*

"I'm going to record this meeting; anything you say can be used against you in a court of law. Of course, right now, you're not under arrest for anything. But our conversation is not privilege like an attorney-client discussion." Brooke figured she would get the formalities out of the way. "Do you understand?"

"I do."

"Okay." Brooke switched on the old tape recorder she had in her desk drawer. She did not want to use the interrogation room for this meeting, so the tape recorder would have to suffice. "Let's start with why we needed to meet right now, tonight."

"Because I knew I wouldn't be followed," Matt answered as he looked at Brooke. She gestured for him to go on. "Catalina's aunt, Maria, spends Sundays at the nursing home with her mother. So, on Sundays, Catalina is busy sleeping with my brother."

Brooke looked up, feeling the shock travel through her. So, he knew. "Catalina is sleeping with your brother?"

"Yes, has been for the better part of a year, I suspect. Ever since we began to drift apart." Matt paused. "It is also the same time that my parents cut my brother Drew off financially."

Brooke stared at Matt, blinking rapidly. "Sorry, I'm trying to digest the bombs you have just dropped. In the interest of time, can you please explain what you think is going on with Catalina and your brother and how it might relate to needing to speak to me? I would rather you just say everything about what you think and know, instead of us going back and forth with questioning." Brooke hoped her direct approach would allow Matt to speak freely.

Matt took a deep breath. "It's probably better to just come out with it, anyway. Catalina suffered from post-partum depression after our son was born. I tried to help, but the stress of being a young family, my long hours, and her depression took its toll on our marriage. We began to fight a lot. This was around the same time my parents had cut my brother off financially. They had been bankrolling him for as long as I can remember. He was constantly getting into debt, and they would have to bail him out. He jumped from job to job to job. They were done enabling him." Matt paused to gather his thoughts.

"Catalina and my brother have always been close. As we drifted apart, she started to disappear for hours on Sundays, saying she was visiting this family member or that family member. Never wanting to take our son, she would tell me that since I worked so much, Sundays were 'my day.'" Matt made air quotes with his fingers. "One Sunday afternoon, I got an angry phone call from one of her uncles, accusing me of hitting her. I have never laid a hand on her, nor would I ever. It just happened to be the same uncle she was supposed to be visiting. When he said she wasn't there, I decided to follow her the next Sunday she went out."

"Why not ask her about all this?" Brooke interrupted.

"Catalina is a pathological liar and a narcissist. I can

see that more clearly now, but I knew then too. There is no winning with her. She would just deny everything. I wanted to see what she was doing. I followed her to her aunt's house. I waited, and a short time after her arrival, my brother pulled up. She opened the door and gave him a very passionate kiss." Matt put his head down, the memory of this event still seeming to affect him.

"Did you confront her?" Brooke was jotting down notes on a legal pad in addition to the recorder.

"No," Matt answered. "Our marriage was over as far as I was concerned. I went to my parents, and they started helping me get things in order to divorce her. Shortly after I finalized my plan, she was picked up by ICE. I was told there were anonymous tips against her. That doesn't make sense to me because she has been here so long and never stepped a toe out of line. I posted the bond. I told her I did not believe she was mentally stable, and that she and we needed counseling for the sake of our son. I told her she could not stay in our apartment because of the way she was acting." Matt paused to allow Brooke to ask any questions.

Brooke looked up from her notepad. "How did she take that?"

"She lost it on me. Three days later, she came to see you with accusations of cheating, abuse, keeping her son from her, and stalking. I believe that the pictures she submitted as evidence are staged, and they are really of my brother." Matt paused again. "I believe Catalina found out I was planning to divorce her and began working with my brother to either try to get me arrested or blackmail me for money."

And there it is, Brooke thought. *The hole, the piece she was missing. Guess Catalina is a good actress after all.*

"Those are pretty big accusations, Matt. To do anything with pressing charges or the law, you need hard evidence, not beliefs." Brooke tried to be matter of fact, hoping he had more concrete evidence. Though, she was also thinking about Dan's last day of discoveries.

"I do. I gave it to my attorney, who said he would get you copies of the phone records, as well as text messaging between my brother Drew, Catalina, and her aunt. Not only do these prove the cheating and blackmail, but also conversations about scam to make fake claims to ICE and frame me for them" Matt gazed at Brooke, now waiting for her to speak.

"You obtained all this legally?" Brooke needed to know. Anything obtained illegally would not hold up in court.

"Yes," Matt answered. "Catalina uses my old phone and phone number. I called my cell provider and asked for the information."

Brooke stopped the recording. "You gave all this to Greg?" Brooke asked.

"I did. I can call him and ask him to send it over to you." Matt started to pull out his phone.

Brooke raised her hand. "No need. I am sure he will. If you have everything you say you do, there is more than enough evidence to press additional charges against Catalina. You already got the protective order, I understand."

"That is what Greg said. I wanted to come down and talk to you personally. I know I can just go to the court, but you helped Catalina first. I wanted to clear my name in case you have to appear in court again for us." Brooke wasn't sure what to think of this statement, other than his attorney probably urged him to visit her as well, to try to prove that she was in the wrong for helping Catalina. More nonsense coming from Greg Levine and his ego.

"One more thing," Brooke turned the tape recorder back on, "you said you believe you are being followed?"

"I am. I have video and photos of Catalina and her aunt following me. That is how I got the protective order." Matt said.

"And they still are?" Brooke asked.

"Yes. The last time I saw either of them was Friday." Matt pulled out his phone to show Brooke a picture of an old green sedan parked a few cars away from where Matt took the photo. When Brooke zoomed into the picture it was clearly Catalina and Aunt Maria.

"Matt, I think you should go down with your attorney on Monday morning and formally press charges. Unless you call 9-1-1 and are in immediate danger, I cannot do that for you," Brooke instructed him, and she was fearful for him. Catalina and her aunt were sounding more dangerous by the minute. "If you see them again, do not hesitate to call 9-1-1."

Matt nodded and stood up.

Brooke outstretched her hand. "I am sorry that this is what you are dealing with. I under—"

Brooke stopped talking. She and Matt turned their attention toward the lobby, where loud yelling had started. Brooke listened. *Is that Spanish?*

Matt looked shocked. His words sent a chill down Brooke's spine. "That's Catalina's voice."

CHAPTER 32

Matt sprinted out of Brooke's office. In the lobby stood Catalina with Aunt Maria, both screaming at the weekend dispatcher in a mix of Spanish and English. He was a new employee, looking like he was right out of high school. He had his hands up, yelling back at the two women to calm down.

"What is going on here?" Brooke shouted at the group. No one paid attention to her. She decided to take a page out of Emma Wright's playbook. She put her two fingers in her mouth and blew. All three stopped and turned to look at Brooke and Matt.

"Sorry, Detective, these two are insisting on speaking to you. I didn't know you were here." The dispatcher was now standing between the foursomes.

"Catalina, what are you doing here?" Matt asked, his tone that of exasperation.

"I should ask you the same thing!" Catalina yelled back at him, anger filling her eyes.

"Let's all just take a breath." Brooke made a sweeping motion with her hands.

"Easy for you to say," Catalina's aunt spat at her.

Brooke turned her attention to the dispatcher. "I'm sorry . . ." His name was on the tip of her tongue.

"Joey," he said.

"Right, sorry." Brooke was trying to figure out what was going on. "Can you tell me what's going on?"

"Why ask him when . . . when *estamos aquí?*" Catalina's aunt once again spit out in broken English. Brooke chose not to acknowledge her, though she knew she was telling her they were standing right there. She was getting sick of Aunt Maria's nastiness.

"These two women just came in a few minutes ago. They walked right past me. When I asked what they were doing, they said they were going to see you. I stopped them, which they did not like, and started shouting at me. That's when you came out." Joey finished, looking from Catalina and Maria to Brooke and finally Matt.

Brooke turned toward the two women. "What can I do for you?" Brooke asked, hoping she did not sound as annoyed as she felt at the unnecessary commotion they were causing.

Catalina shook her head from left to right. "I knew it." She turned and glared at Brooke and Matt.

"Knew what?" Matt crossed his arms. He was not hiding his annoyance at her being here. "Detective Hill, is this considered a violation of the protective order I have against Catalina? Just curious." His tone had changed to a sarcastic and vicious one.

"We can get to that later. Catalina, what are you talking about?" Brooke asked.

"I knew it. Is this why the case was thrown out?" She again was glaring at Matt as her words cut through the air like a sword.

Brooke looked from Matt to Catalina to her aunt. All three were glaring at each other. "What is going on?"

"Don't play dumb, Detective. You are obviously sleeping with my husband." Catalina looked at Brooke and dared her to deny it.

Brooke was at a loss for words. She looked at Matt, who was still glaring, and then to the dispatcher, Joey, who seemed just as shocked as she was.

"Always with your lies. You follow me here? That's how you knew I was talking to the police?" Matt was addressing Catalina.

"I knew you were cheating once again! I'm going to kill you!" Catalina took a step toward Matt, pointing her finger at him.

"Cheating? That's rich coming from you. Tell me, how's my brother doing?" Matt took a step forward, challenging her.

Catalina looked away. "How would I know?" she said dismissively.

"I think we all need to calm down. Catalina, I don't know where you got this accusation from, but it is not accurate." Brooke tried to remain calm. She reached for her hip instinctively. Panic hit Brooke as she realized she left her gun in the glove compartment of her car.

"You are a liar just like him. I know you have been sleeping with him. That is why the judge ruled against me." Catalina turned her icy stare at Brooke.

As Brooke opened her mouth to speak, she heard a voice from behind her.

"That's ridiculous." *Nick?* Brooke's heart seized. Part of her was wondering if this was some crazy dream—the way this was playing out. It was too much like one of those crazy Spanish soap operas Jacs and her love to watch together.

"Nick," she whispered.

He put his hands up in defense. "I went to your house and begged Jacs and Cassie to tell me where you were. It took a while."

"Oh good, *mas policía*," Catalina's Aunt Maria said sarcastically.

"Well, you are at a police station, what did you expect?" Matt let out a nasty laugh.

"I have had about enough of you!" Catalina's aunt took a threatening step forward. She reached into her purse. Gun.

Matt put his hands up as if he was surrendering, his face went white, "Maria."

Nick walked up to stand right next to Brooke and spoke. "I think we all need to calm down. Please, give me the gun. We can sit down right over there and talk this out."

"No," Maria answered. Catalina said something in Spanish, and her aunt answered her. Catalina was the only one who did not seem shocked by this turn of events.

Was this their plan all along? Brooke wondered. She glanced at Nick. He had his hand on his gun in his holster. Brooke said a silent prayer of thanks that he had it on him.

"I think we need to listen to Officer Simons. Maria, please give me the gun." Brooke spoke calmly. "Catalina, please." Brooke looked to Catalina for help with her aunt.

"Why would I help the woman who is sleeping with my husband?" Catalina glared again at Brooke.

"Because threatening an officer can get you jail time, and we don't want that for either of you." Nick looked at both women. Joey, the dispatcher, had moved closer to his desk as the chaos was unfolding. Brooke realized what he was doing. He had been making an all units call for the station.

Sirens could now be heard in the distance. Catalina and her aunt looked at each other as the noise grew nearer. "We need to leave," Catalina said. As Maria turned to look at her, Nick took that as his opportunity to lunge for the gun. It took only seconds for Maria to turn away from Catalina, realize what Nick was doing, and fire the weapon.

CHAPTER 33

"**S**hots fired! I repeat, shots fired. Officer down!" Joey yelled into the radio. Brooke was crouched down next to Nick.

"Nick, Nick!" She was yelling at him after he'd crumbled to the floor.

"Stop yelling," he said as he held his leg, blood seeping through his hands. "God, this hurts."

"Nick—" Brooke started, but he cut her off.

"Go." Nick eyed Brooke. "Go after them, Brooke!"

Brooke stood up. Joey was talking frantically on the phone with 911. Brooke could hear the sirens enter the parking lot. She turned to Matt, whose skin was as white as a ghost.

"Matt!" Brooke yelled. He was staring at Nick in shock. Brooke put both hands on his arms and shook him. "Matt!" He nodded his head and looked at her. "Matt, where do you think they would go?"

"I—I don't know." He peeked at Nick again, seemingly shell-shocked.

"Matt, focus." Brooke moved his face back to her. "I need you to think; where would they go?"

"Um, probably Maria's brother's house. It's in Boyd, Maryland." Matt was blinking hard, trying to snap out of his stupor.

"What car does Maria have? Is it the green sedan from the photos?" Brooke was frantic. She knew every minute counted right now.

"It's a gold Saturn. There is a hole in the front by the passenger side."

Grateful for this information, Brooke turned to Joey. "Joey, I need you to put out on the APB to close exits to 495 going toward Maryland, especially the Telegraph Road exit."

Brooke looked at Nick, who was sitting up now. He had taken off his shirt to wrap it around his leg. "Go," Nick urged through a whisper, indicating he was still in immense pain.

She ran out the door as other officers and the paramedics raced in. She spotted Gavin D'Augusto getting out of his patrol car. "Gavin, I need your keys," she said as they ran toward each other. "Go inside—it's Nick." Without question, he tossed the keys toward her.

Think, Brooke, think. She turned on the patrol car. *If you were them, how would you go?* Back roads. Brooke took a left out of the station parking lot and headed onto one of the lower roads leading to Maryland. She got on the radio. "All units, all units, suspects are headed to the Telegraph Road exit on 495. Check all roads. Suspects are in a gold Saturn with a hole on the passenger side."

A slew of additional calls came in from officers stating their locations. Brooke raced down the side streets without her lights on. She did not want to draw more attention than she already was. She turned down another road and—*There!* Just down the street was the gold Saturn, parked between two cars.

Brooke reversed. *Did they see me?* Just then, another patrol car flew by, and the Saturn began to move at high speed down the street in the opposite direction.

Think Brooke, think! Most of the backroads were a grid system. If she took a left, then a right, she could potentially cut them off. Brooke put the patrol car into drive and sped down the residential street.

Brooke was racing both in the car and her mind. She needed to stop Catalina and her aunt. Brooke sped up, hoping to get ahead of them.

She saw the sign for Hemlock Road. *If I take a left, I might be able to get in front of them.*

The radio was going off, and her attention was tuned to it once again. Now two patrol cars were right behind the gold Saturn. *If I can get in front of them, then there is nowhere to go.*

Brooke took a left. The pursuit was happening two streets down on Rolling Valley Road. She drove to Rolling Valley and looked right. Approaching fast was the gold Saturn with Catalina driving and Maria in the passenger seat. Right behind them were the two police cars, sirens blaring.

Brooke positioned the patrol car to block the road. Two other cars were parked on either side of the road creating a barrier. There was nowhere to go.

The Saturn seemed to speed up, despite the blockade. *They aren't slowing down!* Brooke thought. *Oh my God, they aren't slowing down!*

She was a sitting duck. Brooke unbuckled and went to open the door. The door wouldn't budge, she pushed. It still wouldn't budge. Brooke turned and the Saturn was so close now that Brooke could make out both Catalina and Maria's facial features. Catalina's a mask of horror. Maria's resolute. Brooke closed her eyes and prayed. She tried the driver's side door one last time.

It opened as the Saturn crashed into the passenger side of the car.

CHAPTER 34

White. Bright white. Brooke's eyes were closed and then opened, then closed again. She could only see bright white light, and it gave her a headache. The light reminded her of the overhead fluorescent lights in elementary school. *Where am I?*

She heard voices but none that she recognized. She tried to hear what they were saying. But it sounded like they were underwater—or maybe she was.

Oh, and the pain. The pain set in at that moment, and Brooke felt herself wince. *Where was it coming from?* Her right leg definitely, and her ribs—maybe a few broken?

A warm, tingly feeling came over her. *I need sleep.*

* * *

"How long till she comes to?" Brooke heard Aunt T's voice first.

"I would expect soon. She will be in a fair amount of pain when she wakes. The ribs will heal on their own. Unfortunately, she will be in a boot for the fibula fracture for six weeks and then physical therapy." It was a voice Brooke didn't recognize.

"Well, that's going to piss her off." *Jacs.* Brooke smiled at the sound of her best friend's voice.

"She is just going to have to slow down for a bit." Carol's Southern drawl was unmistakable.

"I don't think the word *slow* is in my sister's vocabulary." *Cassie.* Brooke smiled again.

"Looks like she is waking up now." Benji, the final voice in the crowd of those talking, directed the room to Brooke, who realized then she was lying in a hospital bed.

Brooke opened her eyes and blinked slowly, taking in her surroundings.

"Hi sweetheart." Aunt T walked toward her and gently picked up Brooke's hand. "You're in the hospital."

Brooke went to speak but stopped and touched her neck. Her throat was killing her.

"That would be from the tube. It will start to feel better soon." A man Brooke didn't recognize looked down at her. He was tall, with brown hair and a beard to match. Brooke tried to make out his facial features and the name on his coat, but her eyes wouldn't focus. "Hi, Brooke, I'm Doctor Rhodes."

Brooke smiled, managing to get out a "Nice to meet you" through her scratchy voice.

"You had a pretty bad accident. You broke your fibula, which required surgery, and you have three broken ribs. I can come back on my next rounds and talk about when you will be released and what to expect with recovery. But for now, rest up. Physical therapy will be visiting soon. They are kind people but not super fun. Something tells me you'll do just fine, though." Dr. Rhodes chuckled and shook Brooke's hand. "It was nice to meet you, Detective Hill."

Brooke looked around the room after the doctor left. Aunt T, Cassie, Jacs, Benji, Carol, and Dan were crammed into her small hospital room. She wanted to speak to Dan first.

"Dan, I am so sorry I didn't text you to come back," Brooke said. Her voice was weak, and it still hurt to talk. She touched her throat, looking around for water.

"Sorry—what? Are you serious? I'm sorry I left. I should have stayed to find out who was on the phone. I would have never left had I known." Dan leaned forward as he said this, so he wasn't broadcasting to the people in the hallway. He had to stand in the doorway. The room was not unlike their office at the precinct when it came to size.

Brooke waved her arm as a sign for him to not worry about it. She looked at Aunt T, who was standing next to her bed, still squeezing her hand. "You are not allowed to scare me like this ever again." Her eyes welled up. Brooke squeezed her hand.

"Can I get some water before you yell at me?" She winked to show she was half-kidding.

Jacs offered her the hospital-issued pink plastic water bottle. Brooke nodded her gratitude.

"That was stupid, putting your life on the line to stop

a chase—stupid but brave," Benji said. He was leaning against the windowsill. Brooke nodded. Carol hit her husband's arm. "Not now," she whispered. "And, also, dear, you would have done the same thing," she said with a smile.

"What happened to—" Brooke had to stop talking. The water was not helping the throat pain.

Dan sensed this and finished her sentence for her. "With Catalina and the aunt?"

Brooke nodded. "The aunt is in critical condition in the ICU downstairs. Catalina died shortly after impact."

Brooke closed her eyes. She felt partially responsible for Catalina's death. It was her call to block the street to end the pursuit.

Benji must have read her thoughts. "Don't do that," he said. "Don't you dare think that woman's death is your fault. You stopped a pursuit the way we've all been trained. High-speed chases rarely end well. It was their choice to engage. You saved others' lives by putting your own life at risk."

Brooke knew this, which is why she had made the split-second decision. But she still had a pang of guilt stabbing her in the heart, right next to her broken ribs. Brooke wanted to respond to Benji but knew it wasn't time. She needed something for her throat—a lozenge or something.

"We should all go. Brooke needs to rest," Aunt T said, looking at the group. When she turned back to Brooke, her eyes sparkled with an idea. "How about we let you sleep for a few hours and come back with dinner?"

"Feel like Indian?" Jacs was standing at the end of her hospital bed, a smirk stretching across her face.

Brooke smiled and nodded. It wasn't lost on her that this was supposed to be the plan all along—for yesterday. *Wait, was that yesterday?*

Brooke looked confused for a minute. "What day is it?" she managed to get out.

"Monday," Aunt T answered. "The accident was last night. They put you on some heavy pain meds when you were admitted and then operated this morning." Brooke nodded as Aunt T spoke. "Come on, guys. Let's give her some space to sleep."

Sleep. At the mention of *sleep*, Brooke's eyes felt heavy once again. As everyone said their goodbyes, Brooke's eyelids lowered. By the time they had closed the hospital room door, Brooke was fast asleep.

CHAPTER 35

When Brooke awoke again, she looked around her stark hospital room. Everything slowly came back to her about what had happened. She was trying to focus her eyes when she saw a figure in the corner of her room. He was sitting down, with one leg propped up, looking at her. She blinked hard to determine who it was.

Nick.

She tried to sit up a bit, but the pain in her ribs was too great.

"Don't get up. I can come to you."

Brooke reached out toward the side rail, then the table on the other side of it, in search of her glasses. It was to no avail. But what she saw made her gasp. She closed her eyes tightly. This was not a dream. Nick was there, but he wasn't sitting in a chair in the corner of her room. Nick was in a wheelchair.

He wheeled himself around to the side of her bed, and she opened her eyes. "Nick." Her voice sounded more like herself even though her throat hurt just the same. He grabbed her hand.

"I'm okay. I had surgery last night to remove the bullet,

and I will be released tomorrow." He squeezed her hand more as he spoke. "I'm more worried about you. Brooke, that was dumb—and reckless."

Brooke nodded.

"And also, badass." He smiled at her, then changed his facial expression to a more serious one. "You could have been killed."

"You could have been too." Brooke turned her head toward him. They were speaking to each other as if the past few days of betrayal and pregnancy and cruel words had not existed. But they did exist, and the memory of what had happened between rushed over Brooke. She looked away.

"You should go." She didn't want him to see her cry.

"I can't." Nick's voice was shaky as he spoke. Brooke turned to meet his eyes and saw the tears coming down on his face. "I can't lose you."

"Nick—" Brooke began, but Nick quickly cut her off.

"Tell me you don't love me." His tone was insistent. Laced with desperation. "Say it. You say it, and I will leave."

"It's not about if I love you or not." Brooke shook her head.

"Yes, it is. I firmly believe that if you love me and I love you, we can get through anything." Nick had a hopeful look in his eyes.

Brooke closed her eyes for a moment before speaking. She did love him, but she could not trust him and didn't know if she ever would be able to again. "This isn't going to work, Nick." Brooke turned toward him.

He hung his head and looked at his lap. "I think it can." He looked back up at Brooke, his eyes even more filled with tears. One escaped.

"I'm not the one who broke trust, Nick. I think you would feel differently if you were in my shoes." Seeing Nick cry was making Brooke want to sob, making her throat hurt even more. She placed her hand on her neck and rubbed to help soothe it.

"Do you think you can ever trust me again?" Nick seemed to plead with Brooke to say yes.

"I don't know how to answer that. There is going to be a baby. A daily reminder for me of what happened. I don't know that this is something I can ever move past." Brooke again looked away, now crying softly.

Nick grabbed her hand and put his head on top of it. "I am so sorry, Brooke. I love you so much, and I royally messed up. I hurt you in a way that you should have never been. I am so sorry." His cries were muffled as his head was buried in her sheets and hand.

Brooke placed her hand on top of his head. "Yeah, you hurt me, Nick. I can't forgive that quickly, but we have to both keep moving. You are going to be a dad."

Nick shook his head, even though it was still buried in her sheets and hand. "I can't believe this is happening."

"Me either." Brooke moved her hand from his head as Nick sat up. "But it is."

Nick gazed at Brooke, red-faced from crying. "I am really sorry, Brooke. I am never going to give up hope that you will one day trust me again."

"I can't do this, Nick. All I see when I look at you is the hurt you've caused me. The betrayal. I just can't." Brooke met his eyes as she said this.

Nick looked down and whispered, "I understand."

"Nick," Brooke started, "I think you should go."

"Brooke—"

It was Brooke's turn to cut him off. Her voice was shaking with emotion. "We have both had a lot happen in the past few days—especially these last twenty-four hours—and sitting here looking at each other crying is not going to help. It is not going to change anything. This is the new reality, and we both need to move on."

Silence. Then, "You're right. But I know the minute I walk; I mean roll out that door that this is over." Nick looked toward the door. "What happens now? We just ignore each other?"

"I don't know, but I can't have this play out every time I see you or have to talk to you. We work together." Brooke closed her eyes as she spoke, both from the raw emotional pain and the acute physical pain.

"Have to talk to me . . ." Nick whispered.

"I think you just need to give me—"

Nick interrupted her to complete her thought.

"Space." They said it in unison.

A knock on the door turned their attention in that

direction. "Hi, Detective Hill. I was coming to check on you and go over a few things," Dr. Rhodes said as he looked down at his iPad. He looked up and saw Brooke and Nick's faces. "I can come back if now isn't a good time."

"Now is fine." Brooke looked at Nick. Nick nodded and turned his wheelchair. Before he reached the door, he looked back with tears streaming down his face.

"Bye, Hill."

"Bye, Simons."

CHAPTER 36

Sleep washed over Brooke once more when she was awoken by a knock. The door opened a crack, and Brian poked his head through. "Can I come in?"

Brooke tried to sit up a bit but stopped from the pain. Brian rushed in noticing the anguish on Brooke's face. "Don't sit up." He put the bouquet of pink peonies on the nightstand and dragged one of the hospitals wooden chairs next to her bed. Brooke smiled at him as he touched her face. Brian had another one of his navy suits on.

"You didn't have to get dressed up for me," Brooke's voice was horse as she tried to make a joke.

"I got here as soon as I heard," Brian was loosening the top button of his collar. "Jacs called me."

With the events over the past few days Brooke realized she had never responded to Brian. "Oh my god Brian I am so sorry."

He shook his head. "Don't. It's ok. Jacs told me everything." He grabbed her left hand and squeezed it.

"Everything?" Brooke asked.

"I can't imagine there's more," Brian let out a little chuckle. "Secret baby, shooting, police chase, crash. Did she leave anything out?"

It was a lot over the past few days when you listed it out. "Breakup." Brooke let go of his hand and reached for the glass of water. Brian grabbed it and handed it to her.

"Breakup?" Brian asked as Brooke drank.

"It's over." Brooke handed the cup back to Brian as she said this.

"To be clear, you are talking about him and you not me and you, right?" Brian smiled at her and Brooke knew he was trying to lighten the mood.

"I'm talking about Nick and me." Brooke closed her eyes for a moment. The talking was beginning to strain her voice again.

"I'm sorry that happened." Brooke gave Brian a look that suggested she didn't quite believe what he was saying. "I really am," he continued. "Sure, I wanted you to break up so I could shoot my shot, but not like this. Not for you to be in so much pain."

Brooke closed her eyes again, not from pain but to will the tears to not come. Brian grabbed her hand once more. "Brian, I need some time." She opened her eyes and looked at him.

"I know, and I am here. Brooke, I'm not going anywhere." He was intently looking into her eyes. "Friends?"

Brooke thought for a moment and smiled, "I think I like the idea of kissing you too much to just be friends."

Brian leaned forward and gave her a gentle kiss on her lips. "Me too."

CHAPTER 37

Three weeks later

Brooke pulled into her normal spot at the station. It was surreal to be back here after everything that had happened. She'd spent two weeks adjusting to walking in a boot and dealing with the pain in her ribs, especially with yawning, coughing, or laughing—though she hadn't laughed much. Jacs kept trying, though.

She balanced on her right leg and got her crutches out of her car, still not able to put her full weight on her leg. Brooke was surprised at how quickly she remembered how to use them. It had been over twenty years since she'd broken her leg falling off the monkey bars in elementary school.

Grabbing her crutches, she hobbled into the station and was greeted by June at the door. June gave her a big hug as she spoke. "Oh, Brooke, it is so good to see you!" Brooke wanted to tell her that she was squeezing just a little too hard, but the truth was she missed June and the station immensely while she was home recovering.

June pulled back and looked at her. "You gave us all quite a fright."

"Gave myself one too." Brooke tried to let out a little laugh. "Do you by chance know if Dan has made it in yet?"

"Yes, he is in your office." June looked amused.

"Do I want to ask why you look so pleased?" Brooke smiled as she spoke.

"Last time I poked my head in, he was trying to rearrange your office so you could easily maneuver around." June looked in the direction of their office. "Judging by the amount of curse words that have come out of his mouth the past half-hour, it is not going well at all."

Brooke laughed. "I appreciate his effort. I'll go check on his progress."

Brooke turned and headed toward her office.

June called after her. "It is so good to have you back!"

Dan popped his head out into the hallway when he heard June's voice. "You're early, boss." He looked exhausted and sweaty.

Brooke couldn't help but laugh, even though it hurt like the devil. "Dan, I can figure out a way to maneuver around our office. You don't need to rearrange anything."

"It's been a nightmare, but I have switched our desks. Yours is right when you walk in and mine is opposite. That way you don't have to squeeze by with your crutches to get to your desk." Dan wiped the sweat off his forehead.

"Thank you, partner. I really appreciate it." Brooke was touched by the gesture.

"Let me get settled and then you can catch me up on what I need to know." Brooke hobbled through the doorway to where her desk was now. She noticed the pink peonies in a vase, but no card to be found. She looked back at Dan.

"Brian stopped by this morning," Dan said. Brooke grinned as she smelled the flowers. She could feel her friend and partner staring at her.

Before he got a chance to question her about Brian she asked, "do you know what happened to Aunt Maria?" Brooke realized she'd never heard if the woman made it out of the ICU.

"She is going to pull through, still in the hospital but not the ICU. I also talked to my friend Marcus with ICE. When they came and paid her a visit and threatened deportation, she confessed to making fraudulent claims to ICE and plotting with Catalina to frame Matt for money." Brooke raised her eyebrows at Dan as he spoke. "Marcus says they are still going to deport her." Brooke nodded. She figured as much.

Her phone buzzed in her pocket just as their office phone rang. "I'll get this one." Dan reached for the phone. "This is Beal."

Brooke looked down at her phone. It was Nick. She hadn't heard from him since he'd left her hospital room. *Hey, Hill, heard you are back. Coffee?*

Brooke reread the text message. She was not ready to talk, see, or grab coffee with Nick. She needed a clean break. With tears in her eyes, she opened up his contact information and hit the block number button.

"Hey, boss?" Dan said to get her attention. Brooke turned and grabbed a tissue before facing Dan. He was holding the phone away from his ear. He looked at her with concern but kept talking. "Brian is on the phone. He said we should get down to the courthouse now. Some big celebrity is there, trying to press charges for domestic violence—apparently something happened in our district."

"Tell Brian we'll be right there." Brooke took a deep breath in as Jacs's words rang in her head: *just like with all bad dreams, you have to wake up and start living again.* "Oh and thank him for the flowers." She smiled at what living might be like after this bad dream.

ACKNOWLEDGMENTS

Thank you to Taryn and crew at Typewriter Creative Co. for taking care of my work as if it were their own. Words will never be able to express my gratitude to everyone there who helped me publish this book.

Cortney Donelson, thank you for once again pulling out this story so my work can be the best it can be. Brooke Hill would not exist without your help and guidance.

I would be remiss if I did not acknowledge those most important in my life: my family, both blood and chosen. Thank you. Thank you for your continued support of me on this writing journey and your continued suggestions of characters I should create based on yourselves.

Grace, Jack, Parker, Braden, and Hazel—being your bonus mom has been one of the great honors I have ever received. I may not have been there in the beginning, but I will be there till the very end.

Ethan and Tessa, I am so immensely proud to be your mom. Team Lee forever and always. I love you both to the moon and back and then some.

Joe, I still get butterflies (the good kind) when I call you, my husband. Thank you for being my biggest fan, my constant cheerleader, and most importantly, my best friend. You and me.

And to you, precious reader, for picking this book up, reading it, and hopefully loving it as much as I loved writing it. Thank you.

ABOUT THE AUTHOR

 A.E. Lee started her career in Pennsylvania politics, and while she had hoped it would be everything like her favorite TV show *The West Wing*, she quickly learned art doesn't really mimic life. With long hours, little pay, and even less respect, she decided it was time for a change and embarked on a second career in education.

She is now a beloved sixth-grade teacher in Fairfax County, Virginia, and works tirelessly as a domestic violence advocate in the community. She resides there with her husband and their beautiful children, where she continues to indulge in her passion for writing. Lee is the author of *One of the Lucky Ones, Always, A Collection of Poems,* and the first book in the Brooke Hill series *Bluecoat.* To learn more about A.E. Lee and her work visit her website at authoraelee.com.

www.ingramcontent.com/pod-product-compliance
Lightning Source LLC
Chambersburg PA
CBHW050314110726
47899CB00007B/2242